JUNIOR NOVEL

Adapted by Joe Schreiber

Based on the series created by Jon Favreau
Written by Jon Favreau & Dave Filoni

PRESS
Los Angeles · New York

For information address Disney • Lucasfilm Press, 1200 Grand Central Avenue, Glendale, California 91201.

Printed in the United States of America

First Edition, January 2023

1 3 5 7 9 10 8 6 4 2

FAC-025438-22322

ISBN 978-1-368-09228-9

Library of Congress Control Number on file

Visit the official *Star Wars* website at: www.starwars.com.

A long time ago in a galaxy far,
far away. . . .

STRANGER IN A STRANGE LAND

ONE

THE PALACE WAS NOT EMPTY.

To anyone bold enough to venture down to the throne room once occupied by the mighty Jabba the Hutt, the great hall would have appeared abandoned. But if they dared to venture farther, past the silent bandstand and into one of the upper towers, they would have found a bacta pod, inside of which lay Boba Fett, eyes closed, dreaming.

Fett's memories were still vivid. In them, he was a boy again in the stilt-mounted cities of Kamino, where endless storms whipped the vast planetary ocean in an endless fury of crashing waves. Fett had a flash of Petranaki Arena, the grief and loss he'd felt bending down to pick up the helmet of his father, Jango, who'd fallen there, and seeing his own features reflected in the face shield.

And of course, the Sarlacc pit.

That was where he'd awakened in agonizing pain, surrounded by churning darkness. Gasping for breath, Fett managed to activate the sensor inside his helmet, revealing the slimy intestinal tract that held him captive.

The Sarlacc's gut was a living prison from which there appeared to be no escape. He saw a dead stormtrooper embedded in the pink abdominal wall, already in the process of being broken down by the Sarlacc's digestive enzymes. As his lungs cried for air, Fett reached out and yanked the respirator from the stormtrooper's armor and plugged it into his own helmet. The flow of oxygen helped focus his thoughts, and he swung his fist forward, punching a hole in the raw pink tissue and activating the flamethrower on his wrist. The hole filled with fire. He could feel the creature recoil as he burned a tunnel toward freedom.

Digging his way toward the surface, Fett fought against the weight of exhaustion that threatened to overtake him. Only the promise of fresh air kept him going, and at last he clawed a path to daylight, bursting out onto the blazing surface of the planet. The mouth of the Sarlacc pit gaped open behind him, and next to it, the wreckage of the *Khetanna*, Jabba's once glorious sail barge, left to rust where it had fallen.

Fett was too exhausted to care about either of

these things. Covered with sand and digestive fluids, he dragged himself forward on his hands and knees into the light of the suns. But there was no more strength left in him. He collapsed face-down on the unforgiving sand, surrendering himself to darkness.

The darkness was still there when the Jawas' sand-crawler emerged from the night. Fett lay unconscious as the small hooded forms gathered around him, pulled off his helmet, and began to strip him of his rocket launcher and armor. Their glowing eyes shone with eager curiosity as they rolled his body over, uncertain whether this man they'd found was even alive.

When Fett finally opened his eyes, the Jawas had already found his rifle. On instinct, Fett swung one arm out to grab it, an effort that earned him only a swift blow to the head.

And then again came darkness.

Four figures emerged from the blowing sands, silhouettes advancing cautiously over the dunes toward the motionless body. They were Tuskens, their heads wrapped, mouths and eyes shielded against the environment they had long ago come to regard as their own.

Each of them carried rifles and gaderffii sticks in

front of them in vigilance, but the man on the ground did not appear to present any threat. His skin was sunburned, his lips parched from exposure to the brutality of the desert climate. The Tuskens understood the savageness of this land. If death had not yet claimed this man, it was not for want of trying.

Still, there was no need to take chances. After binding his hands with a rope, the Sand People leaned down and tipped liquid from a black melon into the man's mouth, sprinkling a few drops of moisture between his cracked lips. The black melon, and the milk it contained, was the source of their survival, and they offered only what was needed.

Fett felt the liquid hit his throat, blinked, and started to sit up. His first realization was that his armor and helmet were gone, leaving him exposed. Several hands took hold of him at once, yanking him roughly to his feet. The muscles of his legs didn't seem to be cooperating, as if someone had stolen all his strength along with his armor. Dehydration had left him dizzy, almost too weak to stand, and the sand whipped and stung his face. Squinting into the middle distance, he could make out the shapes of several large fur-covered beasts with impressive curling horns—the banthas that had brought the Tuskens there.

A moment later, the rope jerked again, and Fett staggered to remain upright. He realized that the Tuskens were pulling him behind one of the banthas, forcing him to keep pace with them. He knew that if he fell, they would not stop for him. He stumbled onto one knee, righted himself, and kept going, shoulders aching, arms outstretched as the rope around his wrists creaked and tightened. His head was pounding, his vision blurring, doubling, and he could go no farther. With a groan, he collapsed flat on his face and rolled onto his back, the rope dragging him across the dunes while he stared up at the endless blue sky.

When the Tuskens finally stopped, Fett allowed his head to swing to one side and saw they had arrived near a gathering of tents that marked their encampment. His back throbbed with pain, and his arms and wrists had gone numb from lack of circulation. There were sounds in the distance, the harsh cries of Tusken language, and as figures approached from either side, casting their shadows down on him, Boba Fett felt only gratitude for the shade.

But the sense of gratitude didn't last long. It abruptly ended when the Tuskens tied him to a post in the blazing suns and allowed several of their adolescents to surround him and beat him with gaderffii sticks. An older member of the tribe stood by, watching and sipping from a melon. The beating ended with a boot to his face, knocking him unconscious again.

When Fett woke up, it was night. Fires crackled around the camp, and the desert air had gone cold. Another captive, a red-skinned Rodian, was tethered to a nearby post, and a scaly Tusken watchdog dozed in front of him. Fett turned to look at the Rodian, who gazed back at him, his expression unreadable. Then, with another glance at the reptilian massiff, Fett began to tug on the ropes binding him to the post.

Hearing the sound, the watchdog raised its head and glared at him, then snarled and rose to its feet. Fett jerked harder at the ropes. He was aware of the Rodian watching, waiting to see what would happen. The massiff was moving toward him now, snarling, and Fett could sense its muscles tensing to pounce.

Working furiously, he managed to separate his wrists from their binding just as the animal sprang at him. Fett shoved it to the ground and brought his fists down on top of its head with all his strength, feeling the beast's body go limp beneath him. Then, placing his restraints inside its mouth, he started sawing the rope against its teeth. At last the bonds snapped, and he was free.

After glancing over his shoulder to see if anyone had noticed, Fett turned his attention to the other prisoner.

"Rodian," he said quietly. "Do you want me to cut your bonds?"

The Rodian answered in Huttese, loud enough to draw attention.

"Quiet!" Fett hissed, but it was too late. A nearby Tusken sentry had overheard them and approached with his stick. Fett knocked it from his hand, but the sentry's cry alerted the others, and Fett could already see a group of them charging out of the darkness.

Fett felt his survival instincts kicking in. Still gripping the gaderffii stick, he took off running into the night. He could hear the sound of the watchdog lunging across the sand, already gaining on him. The animal leapt and struck him from behind with tremendous force, knocking him down, and there was a sudden surge of pain as it sank its teeth into his leg. Fett swung the stick at its head, knocking it backward, and sprang to his feet. The massiff snarled and bared its teeth as the two faced off. In the distance, Fett could see the other Tuskens gathered, observing.

After a moment, the watchdog turned and padded back toward the Sand People, who all stood at a distance, staring at Fett, waiting to see what he would do next. He planted his feet and tightened his grip on the gaderffii stick, preparing for some sort of standoff. One member of the group stepped forward with their own weapon in hand.

Slowly, Fett and the Tusken circled each other, and then Fett lunged forward, swinging with all his strength. The Tusken blocked it easily, then went at Fett with a blow to the stomach and another to the head. Shaking it off, Fett swung again, encountering only vacant space—the Tusken's reflexes were lightning fast. The Tusken struck again, knocking Fett's stick away and driving him to his knees, finishing him off with a volley of quick, brutal strikes. As the Tusken turned to walk away, the others moved forward to surround Fett, who had somehow managed to rise up to his hands and knees, only to be knocked flat again.

The last things he saw were the wrapped faces and dark circular eye shields of the Sand People looking down at him before they turned to walk away.

TWO

"WAKE UP, BOSS."

Inside the bacta pod, Boba Fett flicked his eyes open to see Fennec Shand gazing down at him. The former bounty hunter and assassin was already dressed in her standard black uniform and protective gear, her face projecting an attitude of readiness and strength.

Reaching up, Fett tapped a button, draining the fluid from the tank.

"Healing session suspended," an automated voice said as the door of the tank lifted open. Fett removed the respirator from his mouth and sat up while the droid attendant brought him a robe. Fennec was standing by, arms crossed, waiting for him.

"The dreams are back," he said.

"Time to go," Fennec said with her usual directness. "They're lined up to pay respects." She turned and began walking from the chamber. "I'll let them know you're on your way."

Fett got dressed, then put on his boots and stood while the droids put on his Mandalorian armor and wrist gauntlets. One of them handed him his helmet, and Fett placed it over his head.

Moments later, seated on the chair atop the stone plinth that had once served as Jabba's throne, Fett listened to an Aqualish delegate speaking in his own language as he offered a box of credit chips, a tribute to the new daimyo of Tatooine. Fett nodded as he listened, and Fennec stood at his side in silence. When the delegate was finished, he passed the box to an 8D8 droid and bowed his head.

Fett turned to Fennec. "Did you catch any of that?" he asked, keeping his voice low.

"Something about friendship?" Fennec guessed.

Fett sighed. "We really need a protocol droid."

"Presenting Dokk Strassi," 8D8 announced, "leader of the Trandoshan family, protectors of the city center and its business territories."

"That's weird," Fett murmured. "I used to work for him."

"It's even weirder for him," Fennec said.

Dokk Strassi approached. The Trandoshan had

scaly skin and a ridged forehead, and he was carrying something brown and furry in his arms—a pelt, Fett realized. "A thousand tidings to the new daimyo," he said, his voice as silky and ingratiating as Fett remembered.

"It's an honor to be welcomed to Mos Espa by you, Dokk Strassi," Fett said.

Strassi's yellow eyes gleamed as he bowed and spread his arms. "May you never leave Mos Espa," he said, and stepped away slowly.

Fett watched Strassi depart. "Even when a Trandoshan pays you a compliment, it sounds like a threat," he said.

"Presenting his excellency, Mok Shaiz," the 8D8 droid declared, "mayor of Mos Espa and its surrounding plateaus."

But the Twi'lek approaching Fett's throne was quick to correct that statement. "The mayor's majordomo, actually," the Twi'lek said, spreading his hands in supplication.

Fennec frowned. "We were told the mayor was coming to pay tribute."

"Ah, yes, indeed," the majordomo said. "With apologies, I understand how one might draw such a conclusion from the correspondence."

"Very well," Fett said. "Extend my greetings and appreciation for the mayor's tribute."

"Another . . . understandable misunderstanding," the Twi'lek said haltingly. "The, uh, only tribute I bear is the mayor's heartfelt welcome, which I express in his stead."

Fennec gave him a cold look. "So you bring no tribute?"

"The mayor's heartfelt welcome," the majordomo said, "and regrets that he's been drawn away by pressing matters."

Fennec rose to her feet and took a step forward. "If you had spoken such insolence to Jabba, he'd have fed you to his menagerie."

"Apologies, apologies," the Twi'lek said quickly, hands raised, already backing up.

"Tell the mayor I'm here now," Fett said.

"Actually," the Twi'lek said, "there is one other matter—if I may."

Fett regarded him impatiently. "What is it?"

"The matter of tribute."

"I'm confused," Fett said.

Fennec leaned down to whisper in his ear. "He wants you to pay *him*."

"What?" Fett said. "I'm the crime lord. He's supposed to pay *me*."

"Shall I kill him?" Fennec asked.

They both turned to look at the majordomo, who was peering back at them, hands folded in front of him with patient expectancy.

"He works for the mayor," Fett said.

"So that's a no?" Fennec asked, sounding disappointed.

Fett sighed. "That's a no."

Fennec stood upright to address the Twi'lek again. "Lord Fett offers the gift of your leave unmolested," she said.

Having clearly not anticipated this particular response, the majordomo paused for a moment of consideration. "Hm," he said. "Apologies and appreciation. The mayor may take it differently, but I shall indeed convey your sentiment." He began to walk away, then stopped and turned back. "I would not be surprised if you receive another delegation in the near future."

"Keep an eye on that one," Fett said as the Twi'lek departed.

"I keep an eye on everyone," Fennec said.

"Next, Lord Fett." 8D8 spoke up again, and Fett

saw that the droid had ushered two Gamorreans into the throne room for his inspection. The piglike guards, heavily muscled and green-skinned, were shackled with manacles and iron restraints. "These two Gamorreans were once bodyguards to Jabba the Hutt," the droid informed him, "and later Bib Fortuna. They did not surrender even after their patron was killed. They were captured alive as a tribute to you. Their tortured squeals will send a piercing message to all potential challengers to your throne."

Fett spent a moment looking thoughtfully at the two Gamorreans, who seemed resigned to their fate. "I do not torture," he said at last.

"Well, respectfully, Lord Fett," the droid said, "on Tatooine you must project strength if you are to be accepted as a daimyo."

Fett rose to his feet, addressing the two prisoners in front of him. "You were loyal to both your bosses," he said. "Would you be loyal to me if I were to spare you?"

With a grunt, the Gamorreans each took a knee in front of him.

Fennec glanced at Fett and shook her head.

"This is a bad idea," she murmured.

THREE

THE CITY OF MOS ESPA was a teeming network of streets and districts constructed inside a vast crater. Near the center, a tower rose like a central spire around which all the city's energy and momentum seemed to revolve.

In the midst of it, Fett and Fennec walked down the street side by side, with the Gamorrean guards behind them. As they passed the vendors and pedestrians, civilians and droids bustling in all directions, Fennec glanced at Fett.

"You should've let them carry you on a litter," Fennec said.

Fett shook his head. "I'm not being carried around the streets like a useless noble."

"It is a sign of power to the people of Mos Espa," Fennec informed him. "They're used to seeing the

Hutts paraded around the streets. Things would go a lot smoother if you accepted their ways."

Fett didn't reply. They were approaching a lavish establishment at the end of the street, and as they stepped inside, he could hear musicians performing an up-tempo rhythm. On the bandstand, Max Rebo and a Bith musician played for a lively assortment of patrons gathered at the bar and in front of the gaming tables. As Fett and Fennec paused to remove their helmets and descended the stairs, a service droid rolled over with a tray of colorful cocktails and chirped out a hospitable invitation.

"No, we're not here for drinks," Fennec said. "We have business with Garsa Fwip."

A cheer went up from one of the tables as a lucky gambler collected their winnings.

"Looks like business is good," Fett observed.

Two Twi'lek hosts—one green-skinned, the other yellow—employees of the cantina, approached them. "Would you like your helmets serviced and cleaned while you wait for Madam Garsa?"

"No," Fennec said.

"Sure," said Fett. "Here, take both of ours." Glancing at Fennec, he reminded her of what she'd said outside. "Things will go a lot smoother if you accept their ways."

A moment later, Madam Garsa herself glided over from across the room. She was an elegant female Twi'lek with gold skin, her lekku adorned with a lavish headpiece and jewelry. She approached them with an air of unflappable grace. "Welcome to the Sanctuary," she said. "Would you care to partake in any of our sundry offerings?"

"Maybe another time," Fett said. "I'm here to talk business."

"Oh, business it is, then," Garsa said without missing a beat. "Would you like your Gamorreans hosed down and fed while we are sequestered?"

"Oh, no, it's fine. This won't take long," Fett said. "We can do it right here." He glanced at Fennec. "This is Master Assassin Fennec Shand, and I'm Boba Fett. I have replaced Bib Fortuna."

"Apologies," Garsa said. "I didn't see your litter."

"I wasn't carried on a litter," Fett said. "I walk on my own two feet."

She couldn't suppress a bemused chuckle. "Apologies."

"I'm just here to introduce myself," Fett said, "and assure you that your business will continue to thrive under my watchful eye."

Garsa's own eyes gleamed at this promise, and a

faint smile touched the corners of her lips. "Thank you, Lord Fett. And thank you for the gracious introduction, and for making the long journey to visit our establishment. It is our little slice of paradise." Still smiling, she reached out to brush her fingers over his arm. "And you are always welcome, as it is yours now."

As she turned to leave, one of the Twi'lek hosts approached with their helmets. Glancing down, Fett noticed that his helmet was filled with credits.

"Huh." Fennec eyed the coins inside his helmet and then looked at her own. "Yours looks shinier than mine."

As they stepped back into daylight, Fett turned to inspect the thriving intersection in front of them. "Jabba had many vassals," he said. "We've got a lot of ground to cover if we're going to keep his empire intact."

"I can make the rounds without you," Fennec said. "Jabba rarely left his chambers."

"Jabba ruled with fear. I intend to rule with respect."

Fennec fell silent for a moment, considering her response, and then she said, "If I may . . ."

"Speak freely."

"In difficult times, fear is the surer bet."

An instant later, as if to illustrate this point, a red-clad figure sprang down from the rooftop to land directly in front of them. Within seconds, a half dozen others had joined him, the group moving in on Fett and Fennec with a visible air of menace. The assassins wore half masks and body armor and wielded plasma pikes and energy shields. Placing their shields side by side, the red-garbed attackers created a barrier, trapping Fett and Fennec.

Surrounded, Fett and Fennec dropped into defensive positions. Fett thrust his arm outward, firing his flamethrower, but the flames deflected off the energy shields, propelling him backward and knocking loose his helmet full of coins. Nearby Jawas and assorted passersby scrambled to gather the credits as they spilled onto the ground.

At the same time, the ambushers were advancing, attacking them between the barriers of their shields. Fett felt a sharp jolt of pain as one of their energy pikes slashed his arm. He knocked it away and watched the shields press closer, forming a wall through which there was no escape. He and Fennec exchanged glances, and then she sprang upward, propelling her body to deliver an acrobatic kick at the very top of the nearest shield, only to fall back again.

From behind them came a grunt, and Fett looked around to see the Gamorrean bodyguards charging forward, melee weapons in hand. One of them brought down a hatchet-like blade on the assailant in front of him, allowing Fett and Fennec to spring free. Fennec ducked one of the plasma pikes, gripped its hilt, and jammed it into one of the attackers. Spinning, she took another of them out with a lightning-fast kick to the face.

Knocked to his knees, Fett grabbed the pike that was being swung at him, holding on fiercely as the weapon crackled with electricity, and rose to his feet to deliver a decisive series of punches and thrusts that left his attacker unconscious. The Gamorreans charged forward, clearing away the remaining three assassins and sending them scrambling up the walls from which they'd appeared.

Fett aimed his wrist rocket at one of them, firing it and disintegrating the attacker along with part of the balcony behind him. Moving like a blur, Fennec slipped on her helmet and climbed swiftly up the side of the building after the last of them.

"Fennec," Fett said, and she turned to look at him. "Alive."

The two Gamorreans bent down to help him to his feet.

“Get me to the bacta pod,” Fett managed through his teeth.

The two assassins sprinted over the rooftops, leaping across the open spaces with well-trained agility and reflexes. Behind them, Fennec gave chase, spinning herself around a ventilation pipe. One of the assassins flung a metal throwing star at her, and she ducked, cartwheeling backward and leaping from its path.

Turning, the assassins fled in the opposite direction, vaulting between buildings, and rounded the corner only to find Fennec waiting for them, fists up, ready to fight. Caught off guard, they froze and activated their pikes, but without their shields to protect them, they didn’t have the upper hand. Going on the attack, Fennec disarmed both assassins with a precise series of kicks and blows that left them with their backs to the edge of the roof while she held one of their pikes.

For a moment, no one moved, and then she kicked one of the assassins over the edge and pointed the pike at the one who remained, watching as his eyes widened with newfound respect and fear.

Even after all the fights she’d been in, Fennec Shand *never* got tired of seeing that look.

FOUR

BACK AT THE PALACE, the Gamorreans dragged a wounded Boba Fett to the curtained chamber that contained his bacta pod and carefully lowered him inside. One of them inserted the breathing apparatus into Fett's mouth and began to fill the chamber with fluid that would heal his injuries.

As the hood of the bath closed over him, Fett felt the soothing bacta beginning to do its work. He closed his eyes, allowing his thoughts to drift, and the visions began.

In his memory, he was back among the Tuskens, tied to a post in the desert, in the unyielding heat of the day. A young Tusken stood over him with his stick, jabbing at him, as if forcing him to acknowledge the situation he was in. Fett winced from the blow. As before, the pain was intensely familiar; in some ways, the injuries seemed never to have healed in the first place. They were becoming part of him, as permanent as his scars.

He glanced to his left, where the red-skinned Rodian was still tied to the other post. The young Tusken bent to untie him and jerked at the rope around Fett's wrists, urging him to his feet. Slowly, aware of every ache from his last several beatings, Fett managed to stand and follow his youthful jailer through the encampment, his ankle shackled to the Rodian following them, as the young Tusken led them out into the open desert.

What now? he wondered as the chain rattled and clinked beneath him. The dunes kept going as the young Tusken dragged them onward through the heat of the day. One of the massiffs followed them, perhaps hoping for an extra meal at some point, should one of the prisoners be unlucky enough to collapse along the way.

Then in the distance, Fett saw what appeared to be smoke on the horizon. The Tusken was gazing at it, too. Was this their destination? As they drew nearer, Fett, the Rodian, and the Tusken all crouched down to peer over the dunes at what lay beyond.

The smoke was rising from a simple domed building in the distance. Looking more closely, Fett observed a few speeder bikes, a small hydration processor, and several figures walking around the building. Someone dragged a shirtless man out into the daylight. Clearly, this was the man's home, and the invaders had come to take whatever they liked.

After watching a moment, Fett realized that the invaders were Red Nikto—he could make out the horns and spikes sprouting from their leathery skin. One of them kicked the homesteader and knocked him unconscious, and they painted their insignia on the side of the building before getting on their speeder bikes and tearing off.

When they were gone, the young Tusken stood and jerked the rope again. They kept walking, the steps seeming endless and directionless beneath the unchanging skyline. Finally, they stopped, and the young Tusken turned and gestured with his stick, speaking to them in his language.

The Rodian fell to his knees, and Fett gazed at the Tusken. "What?" he said. "What do you want me to do?"

The Tusken screeched and gestured with a scooping motion.

"Dig?" Fett asked. "You want me to dig?"

The Tusken grunted and reached into his bag, pulling out a gourd.

"Dig for that?" Fett said. "All right, you want me to

dig for that." As the Tusken brought the gourd up to his mouth, Fett finally understood. "You want me to dig for *water*."

Breathing heavily, he sank to his knees, plunged both hands beneath the surface, and began shoveling up scoops of hot sand. The Rodian dug alongside him and a moment later, with a cry of success, held up what he'd found. The Tusken took it from him while Fett continued to burrow deeper. Getting the feeling he was being watched, he glanced up to see the massiff glaring at him, the spines of its back jabbing straight up into the air.

"No hard feelings, mate," Fett said, and the thing growled at him.

They kept digging. After a while, the Rodian found another gourd and held it up. Fett shook his head and continued raking and pawing through the sand. He was beginning to think he'd never find anything when his fingers encountered the rounded shape of a black melon, and he lifted it up.

He brought it to his lips, anticipating the liquid within. He was still drinking when the Tusken cried out in anger and charged him, stick raised.

Fett lifted his hand and caught the stick mid-swing.

"Easy, youngling," he warned. "I need some water."

The Tusken took a step back, grunted, and then thrust his hand out, waiting. Reluctantly, Fett handed over the gourd, its precious contents spilling recklessly across the sand.

"I would like a drink," Fett said.

Staring at him, the Tusken held the gourd at arm's length and tipped it over, allowing the liquid to splash down in front of him. Fett stared in disbelief as the watchdog walked over and lapped at the stream. Overhead, the twin suns of Tatooine continued to blaze mercilessly.

Later, the Tusken had fallen asleep next to his watchdog while Fett and the Rodian continued to dig. Fett looked up at his fellow prisoner, still tethered to him with the chain.

"We could've both escaped if you didn't sound the alarm," he said.

The Rodian didn't respond, just turned his back on Fett and continued to dig.

"If you kept your snout closed," Fett continued, "if we can get to Anchorhead, I can get us off world." Anger rising up inside him, he picked up the shackle between them and rattled it. "I could also strangle you with this ankle chain and feed your leg to the watchdog."

The Rodian sat up and spun around, spitting something at him in his own language.

"Oh, *that* you understand," Fett said. "Keep it down. Quiet."

The Rodian went back to digging, and a moment later, he uncovered the hard ridges of something much bigger than a gourd. The Rodian began to move more quickly, dusting and sweeping aside the sand to reveal the huge mass below—a large forked shape covered in some sort of scaly hide. He was still staring at it when the shape erupted from the surface: the huge three-clawed hand of a creature that burst furiously up into the daylight to reveal two sets of arms protruding from its massive torso.

Fett gaped upward as the sand creature towered over them. The beast threw back its head and emitted a primal scream of fury. Then it lunged at the Rodian and snatched him up in one of its hands. Taking a step backward, Fett was instantly aware that he was still chained to the Rodian and there was no means of escape—he and his fellow prisoner were destined to share the same fate. The beast snatched Fett up by the chain, dangling him upside down in midair. Fett could feel the blood rushing to his head, combined with shock and adrenaline and the heat of the day, making everything feel even more unreal.

From behind him, the Tusken's watchdog jumped forward and launched itself at the beast, clamping its jaws onto one of the thing's arms. Batting the massiff away with an effortless sweep of its arm, the creature turned its attention to the Rodian again and, with its upper two arms, plunged him brutally downward into the sand, burying him alive.

The Tusken ran toward the creature and sank his blade into its foot, but that seemed only to further inflame its rage. Slapping Fett aside, it rose to its full height and began to charge the Tusken, who was crab-walking frantically backward as the monster advanced, narrowing the distance between them in mere seconds. It seized the boy's leg, hoisting him up, mouth opening to expose jagged teeth.

From behind, Fett jumped onto the thing's back, swinging the chain down over its neck. He braced himself against its shoulders and pulled as hard as he could against its throat. Bellowing, the beast arched its spine and tried to claw him off, but Fett dug in deeper, twisting the chain, tightening it as the thing's body began to give way, until it fell lifeless to the ground.

When Fett glanced up, the Tusken boy was looking at him. Fett stood, the chains still in his hands, and the youth stared back, an unspoken sense of understanding passing between them. Wiping the sweat from his eyes, Fett lifted the chain from the beast's neck.

Before they left, there was one more thing to take care of.

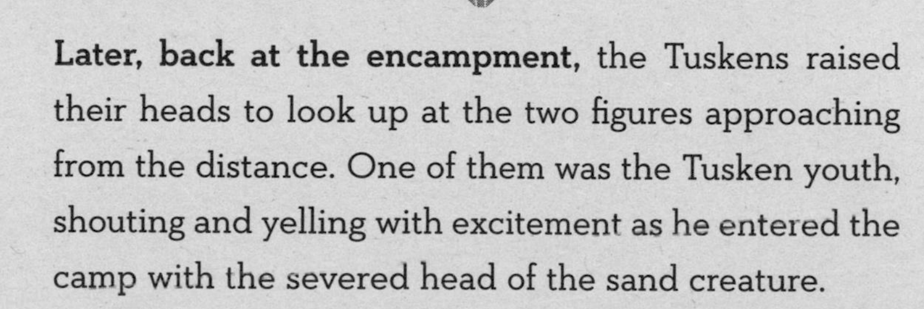

Later, back at the encampment, the Tuskens raised their heads to look up at the two figures approaching from the distance. One of them was the Tusken youth, shouting and yelling with excitement as he entered the camp with the severed head of the sand creature.

Behind him, carrying the shackles that he'd worn out into the desert, was Boba Fett, with the watchdog trotting alongside him. He watched with a smile as the boy continued to display his trophy to the others, reveling in his victory over the monster as the camp surrounded him with congratulations.

Fett looked over, aware that the leader of the Tusken community was standing beside him, also watching.

Without so much as a glance passing between them, the leader held up the gourd that he'd brought with him and handed it to Fett.

Boba Fett took it and drank.

THE TRIBES OF TATOOINE

FIVE

"WHO SENT YOU?" FETT ASKED.

He was sitting in the throne room after his rest in the bacta tank, gazing down at the last of the assassins who had ambushed them on the streets of Mos Espa. As requested, Fennec had brought him in alive.

"What were your orders?" Fett asked. "Speak, prisoner."

The assassin remained silent, his eyes unyielding.

"Well," Fett said, "if he's not going to speak, he no longer needs his head."

"Perhaps he fears the rancor," Fennec said.

The trapdoor sprang open beneath the assassin, plunging him into darkness.

"I was sent by the mayor!" he cried. "Let me out!"

"It's empty," Fennec said, her voice dripping with sarcasm. "Assassin of the Night Wind."

Fennec turned to Fett. "Shall we visit the mayor?"

They brought the prisoner with them in chains straight down the middle of the street of Mos Espa, toward the mayor's office, which was located in a conspicuous white building at the end of the street, a high-profile focal point of the intersection. Fett and Fennec mounted the stone steps leading to the tiled entryway and stepped into the cool interior of the lobby. There was a long reception desk with a clerk in a white tunic and black cap standing behind it. Fennec jerked the chain attached to the assassin, forcing him to his knees in front of the counter as Fett addressed the clerk.

"I am Boba Fett. I'm here to see the mayor."

The clerk regarded him for a moment. "Boba . . . Fett," he repeated thoughtfully, as if trying to attach some significance to the name, and checked the screen in front of him. "Um . . . do you have an appointment?"

"I found one of his stray pets," Fett said, indicating the assassin. "I'm here to return it to its master."

The clerk checked the screen again. "Well, I don't see your name in the schedule, so you'll have to—"

"Pardon the lack of pomp for your entrance." The mayor's Twi'lek majordomo interrupted as he stepped in to take over the conversation from the clerk and offered the same ingratiating smile he'd worn on his visit to Fett's throne room. "However, I did not see your litter arrive." When Fett made no response, he continued, spreading his hands in supplication. "Nevertheless, we are both honored and delighted by your serendipitous visit. However"—the smile faded a bit—"I regret to inform you the mayor is indisposed for the rest of the week, and there are—"

Without a word, Fett and Fennec began to walk around the reception desk.

"This area is restricted," the majordomo said as Fett hit the keypad activating the doorway that led into the inner chamber. "Nope—you're not supposed to . . . Sir, if you would be so kind . . ."

The door opened with a beep, and Fett and Fennec stepped through with their prisoner, the majordomo trailing along behind, still talking as they approached the mayor, Mok Shaiz. Like all of his species, the Ithorian had a long curving neck, and his eyes regarded them warily from either side of his T-shaped head.

"Apologies for the intrusion," the majordomo said. "Terribly sorry, Your Eminence."

Mok Shaiz gazed at them, speaking in Ithorese from the two mouths on either side of his neck as the language device translated his words into Basic: "Who is this who enters unannounced?"

"You know very well who," Fett said.

"It is the new daimyo, Boba Fett, Your Excellence," the majordomo said.

"If you do not know who I am," Fett said, grabbing the chains that held their prisoner and pulling him to the floor, "then why did you send this man to assassinate me?"

"I can assure you, the mayor had nothing to do—"

"He's a member of the Order of the Night Wind," Mok Shaiz said.

"Ah," Fett said, "then you admit it."

Shaiz made an almost offhand gesture to one of the guards standing near the far wall, who immediately drew his rifle and shot the assassin, dropping him to the floor. On instinct, Fett and Fennec raised their weapons and pointed them at the guard, who was now aiming back at them. The assassin's body lay motionless on the ground.

"The Order of the Night Wind are not allowed to operate outside of Hutt Space," Shaiz said, folding his hands in front of him. "Thank you for turning him in." Addressing the majordomo, he continued, "Give this man his reward."

"I am not a bounty hunter," Fett said.

"Is that so?" The mayor seemed dubious. "I've heard otherwise. I know that you sit on the throne of your former employer."

"Bib Fortuna was not my employer."

"It was Jabba the Hutt's throne."

"Yes," Fett said, "and now it is mine." He crossed his arms, his gun lowered. "And I will take this payment as what you should have brought me as tribute." He waited while the Twi'lek majordomo delivered a small sack of credits into Fennec's hand. "You should remember, you serve as long as the daimyo of Tatooine deems it so."

He turned to leave.

"Before you threaten me," Shaiz said, "you should ask yourself—who really sent the Night Wind?"

Fett stopped and looked back.

"I have no motive," Shaiz continued. "As you said, I serve at your pleasure."

"I am not a fool, Mok Shaiz," Fett said, "and those who thought otherwise no longer draw breath."

The mayor blinked at him, moist dark eyes gleaming. "Here is the tribute I offer: some advice. Running a family is more complicated than bounty hunting."

"Is that it?"

"Go to Garsa's Sanctuary," the mayor advised. "You'll see what I speak of."

SIX

THE SANCTUARY WAS AS BUSY as Fett remembered it, full of droids and patrons busily pursuing various pleasures. Music played in the background, along with the casual chatter of customers milling around the floor. Removing his helmet, Fett noticed Garsa looking at him from across the room.

"Ah, what a surprise," Garsa said a bit stiffly as she drew near them. "Thank you for the honor of your patronage, Mr. Fett. Please have a seat at the bar. I'll see if I can free up a table." As she gestured toward the far side of the room, an expression of visible discomfort had already begun creeping onto her face. "Would you care to have a beverage while I sort this out?"

"What's going on here?" Fett asked.

"In what respect?" Garsa inquired.

"Mayor Mok Shaiz sent me here as though there's

something I should know. And now you're sweating like a gumpta on Mustafar."

She raised an eyebrow. "You haven't heard?"

"Heard what?"

"The Twins have laid claim to their late cousin's bequest," Garsa said.

"The Twins are preoccupied with the debauchery of Hutta," Fett said, "to bother with any ambitions on Tatooine."

But he could already hear it—off in the distance, a drum had begun to beat, its steady, ominous thump like the pulse of some great creature. Abruptly, the music inside the Sanctuary lapsed into silence, followed by all conversation as the patrons looked up from what they were doing and directed their attention toward the street.

Fett turned to face the door. The drumbeat was growing louder. He walked up the stairs, putting on his helmet, and stepped outside with Fennec flanking him.

"Watch my back," he said quietly.

She nodded, unslinging her rifle as they entered the street, with the Gamorreans behind them. Up ahead in the intersection, Fett could already see the procession emerging into view. A team of a dozen servants was advancing, with another attendant in front beating a drum as they carried the litter forward.

Fett stopped and waited to meet them. He saw the two Hutts, a brother and sister, atop the litter. The Twins were reclining and looking down at the street below as the litter sagged visibly beneath their collective weight. The female fanned herself while her brother addressed Fett in Huttese.

"Boba Fett. There is business we need to discuss."

"This is my territory," Fett answered in their language.

"This is *Jabba's* territory," the brother said as the drummer in front of them presented a holotablet establishing the Hutts' claim to Tatooine, "and now it is ours."

"I don't care what your tablet says," Fett said, speaking Basic. "This is Mos Espa, and I am daimyo here."

"Oh," the brother said as he used a small, white-furred Hoojib to mop the perspiration from the rolls of flesh around his neck, "is that so?"

He chuckled, and there was a growling sound from behind the procession. Fett glanced over to see a black-haired Wookiee wearing spiked combat armor and holding a blaster rifle walking toward him. Fett recognized the gladiator as Krrsantan, a highly trained fighter and bounty hunter who had honed his skills in the arena of combat. Their paths had crossed before.

"You can bring as many gladiators as you wish," Fett told the Hutts, "but these are not the death pits of Duur, and I am not a sleeping Trandoshan guard. This territory is mine. Now, go back to Nal Hutta."

The sister Hutt continued to fan herself, and whispered something to her brother, who returned his attention to Fett. "You've upset my sister," he said. "I'm more patient than she is. She thinks we should kill you."

At the mention of this threat, Fett heard Fennec activating her rifle, preparing for whatever would happen next, but he kept his own weapon lowered, and his voice remained calm and reasonable.

"Your cousin Jabba is dead," Fett said. "His cowardly majordomo usurped his territory, and then I killed him. All that is his belongs to me now." He paused, staring at the Twins, wanting to make sure that he had their full attention. "Now, your sister is right. If you want it, you'll have to kill me for it."

A palpable feeling of tension hung in the afternoon air. Everyone in the street had stopped to watch this exchange, and they all waited while the sister Hutt murmured again to her brother. Finally, the brother spoke, extending one hand.

"Bloodshed is bad for business," he said. "This can be dealt with later. Sleep lightly, bounty hunter." He gave a signal, and the drummer began to beat out the steady, pounding rhythm that had accompanied their arrival as the litter slowly turned to move away. After a moment, the Wookiee gladiator snarled again and turned to follow while the people in the street watched him go.

Fett took off his helmet, keeping his eye on the procession as it disappeared from view.

"They're Hutts," Fennec said. "We would have to get permission if you want to kill them."

"Maybe it's settled," Fett said.

"You really think so?"

Fett sighed. "No."

SEVEN

THAT EVENING, floating in the bacta pod, Boba Fett continued healing his body while his thoughts cycled back to his memories.

After the incident with the sand creature, his relationship with the Tuskens was different. While they didn't necessarily treat him as an equal, his standing among them had changed in some deeper way, and in the late afternoon, one of the Tuskens had begun training him on how to wield a gaderffii stick.

The warrior demonstrated proper technique for holding the stick, then stepped forward to engage him in sparring practice. Fett tried to imitate the moves of his opponent, only to have the warrior stop and knock the stick from his hands. Then she slapped Fett across the head and yelled at him in Tusken.

"I *am* holding it the same," Fett snapped angrily.

The Tusken shook her head and said something

else, then raised her own stick, and they parried for a few quick moves before the warrior knocked the stick from Fett's hand again and sent it sailing off into the sand. She pointed for Fett to retrieve it.

Fett glared at her, then went to pick up the staff. When he returned, he looked at the warrior waiting for him and drew in a breath.

"Show me," he said.

The afternoon went on, and the lessons continued. After a while, Fett found that the gaderffii stick was becoming more familiar to him. He was able to adjust his grip so the stick felt less like a weapon and more like an extension of himself as he deflected the warrior's moves with greater accuracy through the next round of parrying.

A small group of Tuskens had gathered to watch, along with their watchdogs, one of whom managed to rouse a worrt from the desert sands. The squat, wide-mouthed quadruped hopped off wildly while the massiff gave chase, and as it crested the next dune, one of the Tuskens raised his rifle and fired, hitting it squarely. The other Tuskens ran over to where the creature lay, cheering with enthusiasm at the brief but vigorous hunt.

Then, as quickly as it had started, the cheering and excitement faded. Puzzled, Fett watched as the

Tuskens turned toward the sound of a roar rising in the distance.

Across the sands, something was coming.

Clearly, the Sand People recognized it as a threat. They were already gathering weapons and taking defensive positions behind the dunes. Narrowing his gaze, Fett stared into the distance and saw what was advancing toward them.

The armored hovertrain raced across the sand like a mechanized serpent, its engines roaring as it approached. An instant later, a bolt of blaster fire erupted from the train, hitting a bantha and knocking it down. *FSHEWW!* Another bolt struck a Tusken in the back. Some Tuskens hunkered down behind the dune returned fire with their rifles.

"Come on!" Fett ran forward to help two of the Sand People shelter behind the fallen bantha. "Come on, let's move it! Move! Get down!"

The blaster fire was coming faster, striking on all sides, and a moment later the train was past them, moving away. Coming out from behind the bantha, Fett saw the deadly toll the train had taken in the few seconds of its passing—fallen Tuskens, some injured, some motionless on the ground, while others cried out over the loss of their family and friends.

That night, the camp was filled with the sounds of mourning. Boba Fett helped carry one of the fallen Tuskens, a youngling, to the funeral pyre where the Sand People were laying their dead to rest. As the Tuskens took the small body to place it on the flames, Fett stepped away and drank from a black gourd, his thoughts heavy with the senseless and predatory violence he'd witnessed. Not only did he feel their grief in the encampment, but he felt as if he shared it with them. These were people he'd come to know and respect, who had come to accept him in their community.

And there was something else he shared with them: the deep sense of anger at those who had perpetrated this murderous act, and the need for justice.

Standing in the darkness, gazing into the distance, Fett saw a group of speeder bikes shoot through the night, and an idea occurred to him. He turned and walked back through the camp to find the leader of the community by the funeral pyre.

Gesturing as he spoke, Fett said, "I will stop the train."

The Tusken responded in his own language. "You cannot stop the long speeder."

"I will stop them," Fett repeated, using sign language to clarify his words. "I will take rifle and stick. Be back by morning."

The Nikto biker gang, the Kintan Striders, had taken over Tosche Station, leaving their speeder bikes outside while they drank and caroused inside, much to the dismay of the other patrons. The couple at the corner table, Camie and Fixer, sat in anxious silence while the bikers roared with laughter and slapped each other on the backs. One of the bikers walked over to the frightened couple and helped himself to the food on their table, grabbing one of their drinks and finishing it.

"It's not right," Fixer muttered under his breath.

The biker stopped and looked back. "Did you say something?"

Camie glanced at Fixer, shaking her head, urging him to remain silent, but he stood up, unable to contain his indignation.

"I said it's not right! It's not—"

The other bikers all stopped what they were doing, and one of them grabbed Fixer and slammed him against the wall. The biker raised a stun baton and smashed it against Fixer's chest, firing an electrical current through his body. Fixer cried out in pain while another biker restrained Camie in her seat.

"Leave him alone!" she shouted, but the biker was

already kicking Fixer in the stomach, encouraged by the laughter and cheers of the others. At first none of them noticed the door open behind them.

Boba Fett walked in.

Sensing the arrival of the stranger, the biker stopped beating Fixer, and he and the others all directed their attention to the newcomer, who stood with the gaderffii stick and rifle he'd brought with him. The biker nearest Fett swung his baton, but Fett ducked and slammed the Nikto across the head with the staff. In his peripheral vision he saw another of the bikers raising a blaster, and quickly used his Tusken rifle to blow the Nikto backward across the bar. Fett then lifted the rifle and used it like a club, knocking two of the others into submission.

Across the bar were three more bikers, all poised to attack. Fett gripped the gaderffii stick as he'd been trained to do, unleashing a series of precise thrusts and blows and finishing off the last of the bikers by hurling him through a plate-glass barrier, sending him to the floor in a pile of shattered glass.

Breathing heavily, Fett walked to the bar, picked up a cup, and finished it off in a single gulp. With a nod of appreciation to the bartender, he walked back outside. The speeder bikes were all parked there, and Fett began tethering them together.

It had already been a long night, but his work was far from done.

In the morning, the Tuskens noticed movement on the horizon, heading toward the camp, and sounded an alarm. When they realized who it was, the Sand People lowered their weapons and walked out to meet him. The clump of speeder bikes Fett pulled along behind him was an impressive array of equipment.

Fett climbed off the first bike and approached the leader. "A gift for you," he said.

From behind him came a loud crash. Fett turned and saw that several of the Tuskens had already gathered around the bikes. They'd started hitting the chassis with tools and attempting to dismantle the engines.

"Whoa!" Fett said. "Stop, stop, no!" He held up his hands. "Those are mine! Stop!" He gestured at the group. "I will teach you how to ride." He turned toward the leader and gestured with his hands. "This is how we will stop the train."

At first the riding lessons were a mixed success, hindered in part by the communication barrier with the

Tuskens. Sitting astride one bike, Fett gestured over the handlebars. "This makes it go," he said, indicating a forward-pushing motion. Then he drew his hands back. "This makes it stop."

The Tuskens stared blankly at the bike.

"Go, stop," Fett continued, and mimed a riding posture, waiting for some sign of understanding. "Like a bantha."

Silence.

"Maybe not," Fett said, climbing off. "Okay, who wants to go first?"

The Tuskens exchanged glances, and one of them stepped forward. Fett patted the seat. "Okay, sit." As the volunteer settled in place, Fett pointed to the handlebars again. "Okay. Go, stop—"

The Tusken jerked the throttle toward him and immediately flew backward. Watching him go, Fett wondered if this had been a good idea in the first place and, in fact, if he might be leading the entire community to certain death.

After that initial incident, however, things began to go somewhat more smoothly. The Tuskens were willing to learn, and Fett took them out for more practice, allowing them to get a feel for the handling of the bikes. After a while, he started them practicing a jump from the back of one bike to another, an experiment that initially ended up with one Tusken tumbling off the back of the bike and rolling to the ground. To their credit, they were quick to dust themselves off and try again. While they continued riding around the encampment, Fett found the young Tusken and waved him over.

"When the train comes," he told the boy, "I need you to help signal with this." He handed the boy a mirror, demonstrating how it flashed in the light. Quick to understand, the youth took the mirror and ran off.

After what felt like a long interval of practice, their preparations had improved significantly. The Tuskens had reached a point where they could leap from one bike to another without falling off, and Fett finished the afternoon sparring with the Tusken warrior who had been training him in gaderffii stick combat. After a series of parries and thrusts, Fett managed to knock the stick from his opponent's hand. The Tusken warrior surprised him by sweeping his legs out from under him, but when Fett fell, the warrior reached down respectfully to offer a hand to help him to his feet.

Things were looking up.

Then the train returned.

EIGHT

THE SENTRY LET OUT a cry of alarm, and Boba Fett turned to look. A cloud of dust and sand was already rising on the horizon before the hovertrain careened into view.

"Riders to their bikes!" Fett shouted. "Warn the others!"

The Tuskens took up rifles, and the youth Fett had charged to flash a signal with the mirror ran to his post. Fett and the Tuskens he'd trained to ride all settled behind the handlebars of the speeder bikes.

"Riders ready?" Fett asked as he seated himself with a Tusken behind him. Then he pointed. "To the train!"

He pushed the throttle forward, holding on tightly as the desert landscape jumped and became a blur, the hot wind whipping his face in a spray of sand and speed. After all the preparation, it felt good to be moving and taking action. Behind him in the trenches, the rifle-wielding Sand People prepared to open fire.

But the gunners on board the train had already taken notice of them. Hatches slid open in the cars, and blasters fired, their deadly bolts tearing through the air, slamming into a bantha and hitting some of the Tuskens firing back on the train. The train's sharpshooters were skilled and equipped with advanced firepower, and after a moment Fett realized that they were Pykes. He knew that their only hope of stopping such a fierce and relentless enemy would be the close-range combat the bikes would allow them—if they could get that far.

FSSSHEWW! SHHEWW! A Pyke gunner hit one of the speeder bikes, sending it and the riders slamming headlong into the ground. On a nearby hillside, the Tusken boy Fett had sent with the mirror held it up, flashing its reflective surface at the suns, signaling the Tusken snipers who were waiting with rifles in the distance. Blaster bolts flew and crisscrossed with the Pykes' blaster fire in the open terrain, driving up plumes of sand and dust. One of the snipers drew a bead on the Pyke gunner on the train and fired, taking him out.

On the speeder bikes, Fett and the others were racing alongside the train, close enough for the Tuskens to throw grappling hooks and start pulling themselves aboard. If they could just get to the top—

KKCHOW! A Pyke gunner fired on one of the Sand People, hitting him at close range. While three of the Tuskens scrambled up the train's side, a Pyke grabbed the third Tusken by the throat and shoved him backward, leaving him dangling precariously from the side of the train.

Seeing this, Fett dropped back, skimmed in close, and rescued the Tusken, pulling him aboard his speeder bike. The bike's engine was already running hot from a blaster hit it had taken just moments earlier, and Fett could feel his time running out as the available options quickly narrowed to one. Swinging his grappling hook, he flung it up and over, yanking himself and the Tusken upward just seconds before the bike erupted in a fireball.

Pulling themselves to the top of the train, Fett and the Tusken met the other two who were already there waiting for them. Together they began leaping from car to car, heading toward the front of the train. Beneath them, the hovertrain roared onward. A Pyke soldier appeared from a hatchway in front of them, and Fett swung his gaderffii stick, knocking the soldier overboard.

An instant later, he saw a new group of gunners

popping up from the car in front of them, opening fire. He and the Tuskens ducked for cover behind an open hatchway door, but they were pinned down and outnumbered, with no way forward. As the Pyke blaster bolts slammed into the upraised door, Fett kept his head down and tried to think of how they'd get out of this.

In the distance, the final speeder bike approached. Looking over, Fett saw that it was the Tusken who'd been practicing the bike-to-bike jump—she had been his sparring partner and combat instructor back in the camp. She roared up close to the train, braced herself in a crouch, and leapt onto the train, her speeder bike colliding with the car behind her.

KA-TOOOSSSHH!

The train's couplings detonated in a series of deafening explosions, and the rider ducked inside the train. Within seconds she began taking out the Pyke gunners above her, clearing a path for Fett to fight his way toward the engine.

"Stop the train!" Fett shouted at the spidery driver droid behind the throttle.

But the droid had other ideas. After flipping a series of switches, it launched itself through the hatchway of the engine compartment and spiraled out into the desert, where it picked itself up and scuttled away, muttering as it went.

Fett cast an urgent glance at the controls. Sparks were flying from the consoles, and an explosion rocked the control room as the main turbine erupted.

With no other tools at his disposal, he wedged the gaderffii stick beneath the throttle and yanked as hard as he could, throwing all his weight against it. There was a moment of resistance, and something inside the mechanism gave way with a crack. As the repulsorlift failed, the entire train dropped and gouged a deep trench in the sand, grinding finally to a halt.

Later, sitting amid the piles of salvaged weapons and merchandise the Tuskens had looted from the train's cargo hold, Fett took a sip from a black melon and fixed his gaze on the surviving Pyke captives that were kneeling in front of them.

"Who's the leader?" he asked.

There was a pause, and one of the Pykes stood up. Fett waved him forward, and the Pyke drew closer and removed his smooth metal mask, with its dark lenses and breathing filtration system, to expose his face.

"Are you going to kill us?" the Pyke asked.

"That depends on how you answer what I'm about to ask," Fett told him. "Are you carrying spice?"

"What do you mean by 'spice'?"

"Sansanna spice from the slave mines of Kessel," Fett said.

"What does spice look like?"

From inside the cargo hold, two Tuskens brought down a crate and dropped it to the ground. Fett glanced at the orange powder that glittered in the suns and returned his gaze to the Pyke leader.

"Like that," he said, and took another sip from the gourd. "This is not looking good for you."

"We thought you were uncivilized raiders," the Pyke protested. "We were trying to protect our route."

Fett rose to his feet. "These sands are no longer free for you to pass. These people lay ancestral claim to the Dune Sea, and if you are to pass, a toll is to be paid to them. Any death dealt from the passing freighters will be returned tenfold." Walking forward, he kept his gaze locked intently on the Pyke's obsidian eyes. "Now, go back to your syndicate and present these terms. Your lives are a gesture of our civility."

The Pyke nodded.

"Now walk," Fett told him, "single file, in the direction of the high sun. It will lead you to Anchorhead by sunset if you leave now."

"But we'll be killed."

"You now travel under the protection of the Tuskens," Fett said. "No harm will come of you. We will give you each a black melon. You will survive on its milk as these people do." He gestured to the distance. "Now go."

As the Pykes turned to start walking, one of the Tuskens used his stick to smash open a valve on the side of the train. A spray of water jetted out to shower the Sand People, who cried out in surprise and appreciation as they held up buckets to collect it. Across the open space, Fett saw the leader of the community looking over at him.

The leader bowed his head in thanks.

NINE

THAT NIGHT BY THE CAMPFIRE, Fett listened while the Tusken chief spoke to him in a way he never had before, using sign language to illustrate his words.

"Since the oceans dried, we have stayed hidden," the chief said. "Other tribes have survived by killing."

"You shouldn't have to hide," Fett signed back. "You are warriors."

"The offworlders have machines."

"You have machines now, too," Fett replied, "and you know every grain of sand in the Dune Sea."

The chief gazed at him for a moment, then gestured. "I have a gift for you."

"A gift? Why?"

"You are a good guide," the chief said, reaching down to pick up a small basket. "Now this gift will guide you."

Fett didn't know what he expected when he lifted

the basket's lid. "A lizard?" he said, peering at the tiny creature. "Thank you. I will let it guide me."

The chief flicked a small amount of powder in Fett's face, and an instant later, the lizard jumped onto his cheek and crawled up his nose. He blinked and coughed. "I'm sorry," he said. "I think I swallowed it. It's a tricky little bugger."

"It will guide you from inside your head," the chief said.

A moment later, Fett felt his vision beginning to blur as the world around him filled with an eerie, high-pitched ringing. Thunder rumbled in the distance, and he realized he was walking alone through the darkness toward a tree whose sinuous branches were pockmarked with gleaming red eyes. The branches of the tree began to wrap around him like tentacles, and as he groped through them, other images came: the moments inside the Sarlacc pit, and a vision of himself as a small boy watching his father's departure. Fett experienced all the emotions that accompanied these memories, feelings of pain and fear and loss. Before he knew it, the branches drew tighter, strangling him, and he grabbed the curvature of wood in front of him and snapped it, freeing himself with a gasp.

At dawn he returned to the camp, carrying the

branch he'd broken from the tree. The Tuskens met him, and the leader held up the basket he'd presented to Fett the night before. Fett felt something squirming inside his nose, and the lizard jumped out and returned to the basket.

"I thought he was part of the dream," Fett said.

The chief gestured: "Show me the branch."

Inside their tent, the Sand People began wrapping Fett in robes, scarves, and bandages. These were not mere garments, he realized; they represented an aspect of the culture and history of the people. He stood motionless throughout the ceremony, feeling the power of the ancient customs the Tuskens were sharing with him.

When they were finished, the young Tusken and two others led him out of the tent and away from the camp toward a wreck site. Fett watched as one of the Tuskens began cutting the branch into a gaderffii stick. They handed him a set of tools, and Fett used a hammer and chisel to cut notches into the head of the stick. After carving and shaping the wood, they added pieces of metal to the staff, then dipped it into the oven. Last, they fitted the end with sharp metal blades and held it in the fire once more.

It was night when they gathered again by the fire, where the Tuskens were preparing to dance. Using his gaderffii stick, Fett sparred with the others, but this time it felt different, less of an exercise and more of a ritual that connected him to the community. He might have arrived as a captive, but all that had changed. The Tuskens had given him a new identity among them, a new sense of what his life was, and what it meant.

As the flames blazed and crackled, he turned to join them in dancing around the fire.

THE STREETS OF MOS ESPA

TEN

It was only dawn, but the work of being a daimyo wouldn't wait. Boba Fett sat in his throne room with Fennec at his side while 8D8 briefed them using a holomap of the local area.

"And here," the droid said, "you see the businesses that were under the protection of the name that should not be spoken."

"You can say 'Jabba,'" Fett said.

"I was concerned that you would feel insulted," 8D8 said.

"Why would I feel insulted?"

"Because you felt threatened."

Fett sighed. "Well, now I *am* insulted."

"Can you just get on with the briefing?" Fennec asked.

8D8 continued, informing them how the power vacuum after Jabba's death had resulted in Bib Fortuna taking over the role of crime boss. It was during Bib's reign that Mos Espa had been divided among three families: the Trandoshans held the city center, while the Aqualish took the Worker's District, leaving the Klatooinians with the starport and upper sprawl.

"Where does that leave us now?" Fett asked.

The droid considered. "Everyone is waiting to see what kind of leader you are."

"What about the assassins?"

"The mayor has no power," Fennec said. "Somebody else is behind that play."

"The Hutts?"

"Could be," she said.

From the stairway, a Gamorrean guard let out a grunting squeal, and they glanced over. "One of your vassals seeks an audience with you," 8D8 said.

"Send them in," Fett said. "Perhaps we'll learn what's really going on in this murky fen."

The man making his way toward the throne had a gray beard and was dressed in a sleeveless brown tunic. Approaching, he bowed with exaggerated obeisance.

"State your name and business," 8D8 instructed.

"I am Lortha Peel," the man said. "I am a watermonger in the Worker's District."

"What is your petition to Lord Fett?"

"Well, with apologies, sir," Peel began hesitantly, "no one respects you."

"Enough!" 8D8 said.

Fett nodded. "Let him speak."

"Ever since Lord Fortuna was . . . perished," Peel continued, "the streets have turned to chaos."

Fett grunted. "This is the first I'm hearing of it."

"No, it's true." The bearded man pressed on, emboldened by the response. "And I am insulted on your behalf, at the disrespect these urchins are showing you. Especially in light of the, uh, you know"—he paused awkwardly—"the assassination attempt?"

"Thank you for your insight," Fennec said. "We'll look into it."

As the Gamorreans stepped forward to usher him out, Peel raised a hand to stop them. "What of my petition?"

"Go on," Fett said.

"Well, a street gang of insolent youths have been stealing my inventory. Now, this never happened under the other daimyos, and I am insulted on your behalf."

"And your inventory is water?" Fett asked.

"Yes," Peel said. "I broker sales on behalf of the vapor farmers, yes."

"I grew up surrounded by water."

"Yes, well, Tatooine was once completely covered by water. It's fascinating, actually—"

"What is this gang?" Fett interrupted.

"They are half man, half machine," the vendor answered, not bothering to hide his disgust. "They modify their bodies with droid parts to make themselves even more deadly." He put his hands together. "I beseech you, Lord Fett, rid the streets of Mos Espa of this scourge, and I will double my tribute to you."

Fett turned to look at Fennec, already sensing her response. It appeared as though they would soon be paying another visit to Mos Espa.

That night, they found Lortha Peel's so-called urchins gathered around a fire in an alleyway of the Worker's District. Four young people, their faces illuminated in firelight, were drinking and passing around water decanters as Fett and Fennec approached, with the Gamorrean bodyguards bringing up the rear.

"Where'd you get that water?" Fett asked.

A young woman with dark hair and quick, sharp eyes glanced over her shoulder at him. "We stole it," she said.

"That's a crime."

"It's a crime what he charges," one of the others answered.

"Then farm your own water," Fett said.

The young woman made her way over to him. "Look, old man . . ."

"My name is Boba Fett."

"We know who you are," she said dismissively. "Go back to your palace."

"Watch your tongue," Fett said. "I'm the daimyo of this district, and I will bring order."

"You're a crime boss, just like the rest of them."

A man, the one who'd said that the price of water was a crime, joined the woman standing in front of Fett. His cybernetically enhanced right eye shone in the darkness, and the others all turned to face Fett while he spoke. "If you're a daimyo, why'd you let the monger charge a month's wages for a week's water?"

"Not that we have any wages," the girl muttered.

"You live in the Worker's District," Fett said. "You all should be working."

"There is no work, mighty daimyo. Look around you."

Fett approached them and took off his helmet, allowing them to see the expression on his face. "Then you will work for me," he said. "You've got guts, I'll give you that." He looked at the dark-haired woman. "You better fight as good as you talk *dank*."

"No, no, *no*!" Lortha Peel emerged from a doorway up the alley, where he'd obviously been eavesdropping on the conversation, his face stricken with outrage at this unexpected turn of events. "They stole from me! And you're just going to let them off?"

"What do they owe you?" Fett asked.

"Thirteen hundred credits."

"For water?" Fett asked, incredulous. He glanced at Fennec. "Give him five hundred." As the merchant began to protest, Fett gave him a cold look that indicated the matter was settled. "Take the five hundred—if you want to continue to do business in my territory. And cut your prices." He turned to the youths. "The rest of you, gather up your gak, follow me."

After a moment, the group got on their grav scoots to follow.

ELEVEN

IN THE NIGHT, inside his bacta pod, Boba Fett lay dreaming.

Thunder rumbled, and the waves beneath Tipoca City roared and swelled. He was a boy again, standing by the window overlooking the stormy whitecaps as his father's ship flew off in the distance, leaving only his reflection peering back at him in the dark glass.

Then the vision changed, and he was sitting astride a bantha, wrapped in the robes the Sand People had given him, preparing to set out across the Dune Sea. The ride across the desert was long and hot, but he'd grown accustomed to the arid environment and the steady pace of the pack animal beneath him.

When he reached the spaceport, Fett approached two Jawas. "Where do the Pykes do their business in Mos Eisley?"

They pointed down the street, and Fett rode past

the stormtrooper helmets on newly mounted spikes jutting up from the ground. He tethered the bantha outside a building guarded by two Pykes and addressed the guard at the door.

"I have business with the Pyke Syndicate," Fett said.

The sentry nodded, allowing him in, and Fett stepped inside, then descended the stairs to the shadowy recesses below. A Pyke leader was seated in front of him, dressed in a dark blue uniform adorned with gold brocade, swirling liquid in a glass. "Please, come in. Have a seat."

"You received my message?" Fett asked.

"Protection arrangements are all part of doing business in the Outer Rim," the leader said.

"Very well. I'll take payment, be on my way."

"I've spoken to my superiors on Oba Diah," the Pyke said, "and they are unwilling to pay protection to more than one party."

Fett nodded. "We are one party. I'm collecting on behalf of the Tuskens of the Dune Sea."

"The Kintan Striders have already collected protection money for the same territory you lay claim to."

"You don't have to pay that speeder bike gang," Fett told him. "We far outnumber them. The sands have belonged to the Tuskens since the oceans dried."

“We are happy to do business with either party,” the Pyke said, reasonably enough. “But we do not want to be taken advantage of by paying protection to both. I’m sure you understand.”

“I will resolve this,” Fett said. “You will not hear from the Nikto sand riders again.”

As he rode back to the Tusken encampment, he sensed that something was amiss. There was black smoke rising from the camp. After dismounting from the bantha, Fett began running down the dune toward the settlement to see what had happened.

He stopped and felt his heart sink. Someone had attacked the camp, and what they’d left behind was nothing less than a complete slaughter. Banthas lay dead, and the tents and settlement had been destroyed and burned. As he walked among the smoking wreckage, Fett looked upon the bodies of the fallen—the Sand People who had taken him in and accepted him as one of their own. Their bodies lay strewn across the hard ground, lives snuffed out by the murderers who’d perpetrated this atrocity.

A few steps later, he stopped walking, eyes fixed on the tent in front of him. Painted on its outer flap was an insignia he remembered seeing before, on that day when the Tusken youth had first led him and the Rodian prisoner into the desert. They'd seen a homestead under attack that afternoon by a group of Nikto sand riders, and they'd left that same symbol painted in the wake of their attack.

That night, as Fett gathered the bodies and started the funeral pyre burning, he brought out the gaderffii stick he had helped make and knelt down before the flames in a show of respect. With the fire still crackling, he and the bantha started their long trek toward whatever lay ahead.

TWELVE

BOBA FETT WAS STILL LOST in these visions from the past when a snarling growl cut through the depths of memory, jolting him into the present. All at once he felt the door of the bacta tank being yanked open above him. The shock of the assault caught him completely off guard, and by the time he had a chance to react, it was already too late.

His attacker seized him around the throat, yanked him loose, and flung him across the room. Fett tumbled, still wet from the tank, and skidded across the floor. As he sat up, his head cleared and he realized it was Krrsantan, the gladiator who had come with the Hutts into the streets of Mos Espa, outside Garsa's Sanctuary.

As he started to stand, Krrsantan picked him up and hurled him into the wall with a deafening crash. Fett grabbed his gaderffii stick and slammed it into his attacker, but the gladiator grabbed him with effortless strength and hoisted him off the ground. As Fett punched Krrsantan in the head, the Wookiee bit him. A dagger of pain shot down Fett's hand and wrist as the sharp teeth cut through his flesh. Krrsantan's grip tightened, bending Fett's spine and crushing his ribs, and he felt his strength collapsing in the powerful arms. Darkness encircled his vision, tightening into unconsciousness, and he couldn't breathe.

Then all at once, Krrsantan's grip released. Falling to the ground, Fett realized they were no longer alone in the room. The youths he'd hired to work for him had just arrived, and the dark-haired girl—she'd introduced herself as Drash—had jammed her blade into the Wookiee's back. The others were circling their opponent, weapons at the ready.

There was a sharp crackle as one of them flipped an electric flail, but the Wookiee fought the others off and swung at Fett, sending him staggering into the bacta pod.

Alerted by the activity, the two Gamorrean bodyguards hurried into the chamber. With a vicious snarl, Krrsantan charged and knocked them down, and the fight dragged its way down into the throne room, where the gladiator took a bite out of one of the bodyguard's shoulders, eliciting a shriek of pain. Drash, Skad, and the others ran down the steps to surround the tireless Wookiee, but before they could act, Fennec Shand appeared on the other side of the room.

"Stay back!" Fennec ordered, and reached out to hit the switch activating the trapdoor. The door swung open, and Krrsantan fell through the opening, catching himself at the last second. He hung by one hand, dangling from the edge, snarling and glaring up at them. Fennec pulled a knife and flicked it downward into the Wookiee's hand, dislodging his grip and sending the fighter plummeting into the darkness of the rancor's paddock.

For a moment everyone stood catching their breath. Fett put on a robe and assessed the damage the would-be assassin had left behind. One of the bodyguards was badly wounded from the Wookiee bite.

"Get him to my bacta tank," he said.

Down in the darkness, the Wookiee roared.

Later, seated at the end of a long banquet table, Fennec put her feet up and took an appreciative bite of a perfectly roasted drumstick. At the other end, Boba Fett sat pensively, not eating. When the astromech droid rolled over to him with yet another platter, he waved it away with an impatient flick of the hand.

"Enough food," Fett said. "Go help with the patrol."

"You're the head of a family," Fennec said. "You should enjoy the trappings."

"I need to respond," Fett told her. "Everyone is watching. Waiting for me to make the next move."

"Have some food."

Fett shook his head. "I have to send a message."

"You already did," Fennec observed. "They sent Krrsantan to kill you. Now he's locked up in your dungeon. I say wait for them to show their hand."

"These are Hutts," Fett said. "Waiting will only give them the opportunity to strike again."

"Pardon the interruption, Master," 8D8 said from the doorway.

"What is it?" Fett asked.

"The Twins are here." The droid paused, hesitating. "They have brought a gift."

When Fett and Fennec emerged into the daylight with their armor, helmets, and weapons, Fett saw the Hutts'

litter in front of the palace, held up by a team of servants dressed in red-and-white uniforms.

"We have come to apologize," the Hutt brother said.

Fett gazed at them suspiciously. "Go on."

"We sent Krrsantan to kill you," the sister said.

"We are sorry," her brother answered. "Please accept this gift as restitution."

Fett looked over at the repulsorlift sled gliding toward them, and the enormous creature chained on top of it. The gift the Hutts had brought him was a young rancor, and the human keeper who accompanied it directed the sled closer to the gates. Fett regarded the beast and its keeper for a moment before returning his attention to the Hutt twins.

"Clear off Tatooine," he told them, "and I will consider a truce."

"We will do just that," the sister Hutt said, "but for a different reason. There is something you should know."

"Say your piece."

"We were both lied to," the brother said. "This territory has already been promised to another syndicate."

"Promised by who?"

"That spineless mayor Mok Shaiz," the sister answered.

"And what of the Hutts?" Fett inquired.

"We are going back to Hutta," the brother said. "We don't want war." He chortled. "Bad for business."

As Fett processed all they had said to him and what it might mean for his role as daimyo, he heard the rattle of chains behind him. His bodyguards brought forth Krrsantan in shackles. The Wookiee still looked outraged from being plunged into the rancor's den.

"Here is your prisoner," Fett said. "I offer him back if you renounce all claims to Jabba's legacy on Tatooine."

"We are leaving," the brother said, "and recommend you do the same."

"Tatooine is a worthless rock," his sister agreed. "Sell the Wookiee back to the gladiators."

"He is our tribute to you," the brother said.

The parlay was over. As the Hutts' attendants began turning their litter around and bearing it away, Boba Fett glanced at the Gamorrean holding Krrsantan's chains.

"Release him," Fett said, and faced the Wookiee. "No hard feelings. It's just business." As the bodyguards finished removing Krrsantan's manacles, Fett offered him a final word of advice. "Take it from an ex-bounty hunter: Don't work for scugholes. It's not worth it."

With a growl, the Wookiee turned and began loping away.

"You sure that was a good idea?" Fennec asked, watching Krrsantan go.

"It was either that or kill him," Fett said.

She paused. "Do you believe what the Hutts said?"

"I have no reason to believe them," Fett said. "They would benefit from their enemies fighting one another."

"I'll arrange a meeting with the mayor." She turned her head to assess the rancor, wrapped in chains and sprawled on the floating sled, and nodded appreciatively. "Quite the gift."

Down in the darkness beneath the throne room, the rancor lay motionless with a pair of blinders covering its eyes. It was growling softly and not moving. Fett and the keeper walked alongside it, observing the creature in its melancholy state.

"Why does it just lie there?" Fett asked.

"It's depressed," the keeper said.

Fett turned to look at him, surprised. "This beast can feel such things?"

"Rancor are emotionally complex creatures."

"Why does it wear blinders?"

"This one is a calf," said the keeper. "It was bred from champions for fighting. I saved this one for myself to train. It imprints on the first human it sees." He drew in a breath. "Now that we've arrived, I will begin its training."

Fett gestured to the beast, extending one hand to touch it. "Can I?"

"Yes, go ahead," the keeper said. "They're quite peaceful unless threatened."

Fett walked over and placed his hand on the rancor's head, and it growled louder, acknowledging this new disturbance.

"Whoa, easy. Easy, boy." Fett rubbed his palm against the rough, leathery hide and felt the creature settling at the calm sound of his voice. "I think it likes this."

"It does," the keeper agreed.

"I will spend more time with it."

"You should," the keeper told him. "They can become very loving."

Fett continued to stroke the rancor's face. "I thought they were bred just to fight."

"They're powerful fighters," the keeper said, "so that is what most know. But they form strong bonds with their owners. It is said that the witches of Dathomir even rode them through the forests and fens."

Fett thought for a moment and made up his mind. "I want to learn to ride this one."

"You *what*?" the keeper said, taken aback.

"I want to ride it," Fett said. "I've ridden beasts ten times its size. Teach me."

For the first time, the keeper appeared hesitant. "It will take a tremendous amount of discipline," he said.

Fett nodded. "We begin today." He returned his attention to the rancor. "Yes," he said, stroking its great head. "Now, what are we going to call you?"

The keeper positioned himself in front of the creature's head. "Stand here," he said. When Fett had taken his place, the keeper approached the rancor and removed the blinders, and for the first time, Fett saw the creature's small black eyes, meeting his own. He sensed a deep gentleness in those eyes and recognized an immediate trust.

"Easy, boy," Fett said as he reached up to scratch it. "Easy." As the thing grumbled its appreciation at this physical contact, Fett smiled and continued to rub the side of its head. "Is this the spot? Oh, yes, you like this."

"Excuse me, Lord Fett," 8D8's mechanized voice cut in.

"Not now. I'm busy."

"We heard back from the mayor's office," the droid continued, ignoring the command. "He remains completely unavailable for the next twenty days."

Fett turned to the keeper. "Feed the rancor," he said. "Give it a full ronto carcass from the larder." He patted its head again. "I think it's hungry." He walked past 8D8 on his way to the door. "Tell Fennec to suit up," he commanded. "We're not waiting for an appointment."

As he left the rancor's den, the keeper turned to the creature lying next to him.

"Don't worry," the keeper said. "He'll be back."

THIRTEEN

FETT AND FENNEC walked toward the mayor's office in Mos Espa with the group of four cybernetically modified youths riding along behind them on multi-colored grav scoots. As Fett entered the lobby, he saw the mayor's Twi'lek majordomo behind the reception desk, eyeing him with unmistakable anxiety.

"We're here to see the mayor," Fett said.

"Yes, indeed," the Twi'lek said. "Unfortunately, uh, Mayor Mok Shaiz's schedule is a bit complicated—"

"If you wish to continue breathing," Fennec said, "I advise you to weigh your next words carefully."

"Hm," the majordomo said, visibly uncomfortable. "Actually, now that you mention it, I may be able to rearrange some of the appointments. So if you'll excuse me, I'll see what I'm able to do." He pivoted and strode through the door behind the counter.

The switch next to the door blinked and turned red. "Did he just lock the door?" Fett asked.

"Dank farrik!" Fennec cursed, and they ran out of the building in time to see the majordomo whipping around the corner in a landspeeder.

"Get him!" Fennec shouted to the four Mods waiting down by the front steps. Drash, Skad, and the others quickly mounted their scoots. The Mods pursued the speeder down the street and around the corner until they forced the majordomo to spin into a stand of ripe meiloorun fruits, where the speeder crashed to a halt.

While the majordomo sat half-submerged in fruits, struggling to restart the speeder's stalled engine, Fett used his jet pack to descend to the ground to confront the majordomo.

"Where is the mayor?"

"He's with the Pykes," the Twi'lek said. "The mayor's gone. He's working with the Pykes."

"Is he?" Fett looked at the Twi'lek closely, allowing this information to sink in. As disturbing as it was, it wasn't exactly a surprise.

The starliner docking at Mos Espa's spaceport had just settled to the landing bay, and an entourage of Pykes strode down the ramp, unaware that they were being watched. Skad, observing it all from his grav scoot, flipped the mirror up, hit the throttle, and rode off. Within moments he'd located a hologram station and reached out to Fett at his palace to make a report.

"Are you sure?" Fennec asked.

"I know a Pyke when I see one," Skad said.

"How many?" Fett asked.

"I saw a dozen at least."

Fennec turned to Fett. "They arrived on the starliner."

"Good work," Fett told Skad. "Keep an eye on them." Then, realizing what he'd said, he added: "Sorry, it's just an expression."

Skad smiled. "You don't have to be sorry, mate," he said, gesturing to the cybernetic modification on the right side of his face. "I paid a lot for this. I'm proud of my eye."

"Let us know what you see," Fennec told him. Deactivating the holo, she returned her attention to Fett. "These are just a first wave. They're going to war."

"Then we will be ready," Boba Fett said.

THE GATHERING STORM

FOURTEEN

THAT NIGHT, as he had many times in the past, Boba Fett returned to his bacta pod.

His memory took him back to the terrible moment when he'd ridden away from the Sand People's encampment and the senseless brutality that had occurred there. Astride a bantha, he had made his way toward Jabba's palace and dismounted to position himself high above the main gate. From this vantage point, the scope of his cycler rifle allowed him a clear view of the sentries positioned outside. Fett lowered the gun and then returned to the bantha.

"Not today, old girl," he said. "There's too many guards. Let's get something to eat."

That night in the desert, roasting a chunk of meat over an open flame, he noticed the bantha licking its lips. "There you go," Fett said, tossing it a scrap. "Enjoy."

The beast smacked its lips, devouring the morsel

with a grunt of satisfaction. As they settled in for the night, Fett noticed a bright light in the distance, rising and arcing in the darkness like a flare. The sight of it snapped him to sudden attention. Such things weren't seen often out there, and it meant he and the bantha weren't alone.

Mounting up, he rode across the sand in the direction of the flare. When he finally got there, he found a woman's body lying on the ground, motionless. Going closer, he saw that she was dressed in black, with the boots, wrist gauntlets, and shoulder pads of a warrior. Someone had left her for dead.

Fett looked more closely at her face, and after a moment he realized who she was: Fennec Shand, the assassin. Lifting her up, Fett placed her on the back of his bantha and began to ride toward Mos Eisley. He had no idea whether she would survive or not, but he had to try. His rescue efforts took him to a mod parlor on the outskirts of the city, a remote establishment where customers could pay to have themselves equipped with cybernetic enhancements. Pulsating electronic music filled the area around the shop. Outside the entrance, a small gathering of modified youths observed Fett carrying Shand's unconscious body into the parlor.

The open space was illuminated by fluorescent

lamps that shone down on an impressive array of customized electronics and surgical gear. On a nearby table, a mod artist was using a set of precision tools to implant a new robotic modification at the base of a customer's spine. Fett placed Shand's body on an empty bed and waited for the Modifier to look over his shoulder at him.

"Aren't you a little old to be here?"

"She needs modification," Fett said.

"No walk-ins," the Modifier said. "Appointment only."

"This woman is about to die," Fett said, dropping a clinking bag of credits next to the workstation. The proprietor looked at the sack of credits, then up at Fett.

"Well," he said, "you should've started with that."

Tools whirred and a thin tendril of smoke rose in the air as the artist set about his work, using a surgical saw and cauterizing torch to equip Shand's body with the enhancements and sensors that would keep her alive. Finishing, he sat up.

"It's done," he said.

Fett looked down at the exposed biomechanical equipment in Shand's abdomen. "Aren't you going to close her up?"

"And cover all that beautiful machinery?" The artist smiled.

Fett sat by the fire in the faint light of dawn with the bantha tethered nearby, waiting for Shand to regain consciousness. There was no telling how she might react when she woke up.

When she finally began to stir, the expression on her face was a mixture of pain and confusion. She looked at him, immediately on guard.

"What happened?" she asked.

"You were dying of a gut shot," Fett said. "I saved your life."

Fennec looked down at herself, where half the muscle and tissue of her lower torso had been partially replaced with strange-looking machinery, an assortment of wires and metallic parts. "What did you do to me?"

"I brought you to a mod parlor on the outskirts of Mos Eisley," Fett told her. "It was the best I could do under the circumstances."

She coughed and groaned with pain. Her mouth was parched, and her throat ached from the lack of hydration.

"Take the black melon," the man said. "It will help you recover."

Wincing, she picked up the fruit he'd placed in front of her.

"It takes some getting used to," he said. "In time you start to crave it." He waited while she gulped the milk of the melon. "You are Master Assassin Fennec Shand of the Mid Rim."

Fennec rolled onto her side to look back at him, realizing why the stranger had bothered to save her life. "I take it I'm worth more alive, huh?"

"You are."

"I'll pay double my bounty."

"I don't want money," the man said.

She gazed at him warily. "Who are you?"

"I am Boba Fett."

She frowned. "Boba is dead."

"I was left for dead on the sands of Tatooine," he said, "like you. I was rescued by the Sand People. They took me in and treated me as one of their own. I tried to help them." He paused, remembering. "Instead I got them massacred by Nikto speed bikers."

"Speed bikers defeated Tuskens?" Fennec asked with evident skepticism. "That's highly unlikely."

"I want you to help me," Fett said. "Help me recover my Firespray gunship."

Fennec sighed. "Where is it?"

"Jabba the Hutt's palace."

Fennec considered the proposal. "Bib Fortuna took over his territory," she said, "and now he rules from that palace. If the ship is yours, why don't you just ask for it back?"

"Because I might not like the answer," Fett said. "Without my armor, I'm less persuasive."

"If I help you, my debt is paid."

Fett nodded. "If that is what you wish."

They rode through the heat of the day, arriving outside the gates of Jabba's palace under cover of darkness. Hidden in the crags of the canyon high above the fortress, Fennec used the scope of her sniper rifle to peer down at the area outside the palace gate.

"Your ship's there, all right," she said, focusing on the Firespray vessel. "Any idea how many guards?"

"I can't tell," Fett said. "The gate opens, some come out, some go in."

"Let's take a closer look." Fennec activated a tiny surveillance remote and released it to fly over the area. The remote flew unnoticed above the rising gate and glided silently through a series of hallways inside the palace, past Jabba's kitchen, and behind an unsuspecting Gamorrean guard before dipping down the curved staircase leading to the throne room. Its three red eyes recorded everything it encountered in its hovering flight.

Up by their campfire, Fennec was cleaning her rifle as Fett approached the bantha that had carried them there. "It's time," he told the animal. "It's time to say farewell, my friend. You served me well."

Bellowing sadly, the animal licked his face.

"Yes, I know," Fett said as he gave the creature a fond pat. "I'm gonna miss you, old girl." He finished untethering it. "Now go. Find other banthas. Make baby banthas. Go!" He tossed a scrap of meat out toward the darkness, coaxing the bantha to go after it. "You're free to roam the Dune Sea."

"Shouldn't you wait until we get your ship back before you do that?" Fennec asked as she snapped the scope onto her rifle.

"Why?" Fett said. "Either I get it or I die." He settled himself on the opposite side of the fire. "Soon you'll be free, too."

"What's next for you?" Fennec asked.

"I'm going to find my armor," Fett said, jabbing at the fire with a stick. "And then I'm going to kill that bloated pig who double-crossed me and take his throne."

Fennec gave him a surprised look. "You want to head a gotra?" she asked, using the term for an organized crime group.

"Why not?"

"You're a hunter."

"I'm tired of working for idiots who are gonna get me killed," Fett said. Across the crackling flames, he raised his eyes to meet hers. "The Tuskens took me in. Made me part of their tribe. I was ready to leave hunting behind."

"People like us don't get to decide when we're finished," Fennec said. Snapping the last piece of her rifle in place, she saw the glowing red light of the remote flying back toward her. "Ah." After holding out her palm so the remote could land on it, Fennec pressed a switch and the remote projected a wide fan of light, a high-resolution hologram of Fett's ship.

"There she is," Fett said. He and Fennec looked at the clusters of small red shapes indicating the life-forms surrounding the ship—twenty or more. "There are too many guards."

"Then we time their patrol," Fennec said, "and go in quiet."

Fett looked at her and nodded. That would be the plan.

FIFTEEN

THEY MOVED IN SILENCE over the terrain toward a metal grate outside the palace. Approaching the set of metal bars, Fennec used a laser torch to cut through two of them, then knocked the broken bars aside and crept into the sewer. It wasn't exactly the most imposing way to make an entrance, but it was their only option. With a deep breath, Fett followed.

In Jabba's kitchen, two chef droids were at work preparing a meal. One of them was using its multitude of limbs to chop and dice vegetables while the other stirred a large simmering cauldron, using a spoon to knock one of the livelier ingredients back into the pot when it tried to escape. There was a rustling sound from somewhere beneath the kitchen floor, and the metal grate shifted and started to lift up.

"What was that?" the chopping droid asked.

"I don't know," the other replied. "More rats?"

"Go find it," the chef droid said. "I will contact the ratcatcher."

The droid that had been stirring the pot went over to investigate and saw that the grate on the floor had been moved. "I don't think it was a rat. Call secur—"

Thwack! Boba Fett jumped out and slammed the robot across the head with his gaderffii stick, then stepped toward the other droid, which stopped chopping vegetables and rounded the counter, raising its arms to reveal an impressive array of spinning cutlery. As Fett drew nearer, the knives spun faster in a blur of razor-sharp metal.

Fennec popped up behind the droid and slit the mechanical coupling device that connected its head to its main torso unit. Its head fell off, landing on a bed of chopped greens.

"No one sounded the alarm," Fett said.

"Let's get to the hangar."

"We'll slip past the guards."

They froze at the sound of footsteps and spun around to see a small green-eyed LEP service droid walking around the corner, carrying a net to catch rats. The droid stopped and muttered to itself, inspecting the kitchen, then turned to look up at Fett and Fennec.

Fett swung at it, but the droid ducked and scurried

across the kitchen and under the table, knocking over a pile of pots and sending them clattering to the floor. It sprang from the top of the stove down through a heating conduit beneath the kitchen range, but Fett finally managed to corner it in the doorway and grabbed it by the neck.

"Gotcha." He held up the droid. "Do you know who I am? I am Boba Fett."

Terrified, the LEP droid began to sob. Its upper antenna ears sagged in defeat as it reached up to switch itself off. Its eyes went dark.

"Quick little bugger," Fett said, tossing it into an empty pot with a clang.

"Are you finished?" From the doorway, Fennec was watching all this with eyebrows raised. "Can we go now?"

They made their way quickly down to the hangar, and Fett saw his ship waiting for him. There were no guards he could see, and at first it seemed that they might actually get away clean. Then from the shadows came the lumbering footsteps of Gamorrean guards advancing toward them. The Gamorreans were strong but slow-moving. Fett and Fennec each took one of the guards, knocking them out and leaving them unconscious on the floor.

"Good work," Fett said.

She nodded. "Not bad yourself."

Overhead, an alarm began to go off, filling the entire hangar. More guards were charging down the corridor, firing blasters as they ran. Fett and Fennec took cover behind storage barrels along the ship, and Fennec fired back, hitting one of the guards while the others continued shooting.

"You go!" she told Fett. "I'll handle them. Make sure that thing can still fly."

Nodding, Fett scrambled up the side of the ship and climbed into the cockpit, leaning all the way back so he was looking straight up. He could hear the blaster fire outside as the guards exchanged shots with Fennec. Powering up the avionics systems, he saw the familiar display lights brightening as the turbines roared to life.

Down on the hangar floor, Fennec saw more guards racing in to join the firefight. From her hiding place, she spotted a heavy-duty power droid waddling obliviously through the fray. Fennec fired on the droid, scoring a direct hit.

KA-CHOOMM! The droid went up in a ball of flame that threw a half dozen of the closest guards in every direction. She spun, targeting two more guards, watching the ship struggle to lift itself from the floor of the hangar. Her position was increasingly unstable.

Already another detachment of guards was racing in, and she knew she couldn't take them all.

At that moment, Fett hit the ship's thrusters, releasing a tremendous burst of power that scattered the guards. Fennec raced up the gangplank, and there was a crash as the ship slammed into the hangar wall, throwing her down.

"What are you doing?" Fennec shouted.

"We need to get the gate open, but I can't see a thing!" Fett said.

Fennec glanced at the Gamorrean guard who had chased her up the boarding ramp. "A little busy here," she said, swinging a fist into the guard's face. The ship was struggling to get free, plowing through concrete structures, as Fennec spun around to find herself confronted by a Nikto guard who had climbed up on the ship's hull.

The Nikto punched her, and Fennec staggered back as the ship tilted sideways underneath her. "The guns are jammed!" Fett shouted. "I can't get a shot!"

Slamming the Nikto in the stomach, Fennec glanced across the hangar at the counterweight system by the gate. "I've got it. Close the ramp!"

"I hope you know what you're doing," Fett murmured under his breath.

Fennec grabbed the Nikto, flipping him and sending him sliding off the hull of the ship. Then, with the ramp closing beneath her, she raised her rifle and fired at the counterweight, hitting it directly. All around them, metal began to creak, and there was a deep thud as the counterweight dropped, wrenching open the hangar door.

The ship roared from its confines and sailed out into open air, gliding over the planetary surface and away from Jabba's palace.

"Next time," Fennec said as they flew away, "we stick to the plan."

Behind the controls, Fett glanced at her. "Next time?"

"How's the ship?"

"She's in good shape," Fett said. "Just a little rusty."

"There are good mechanics in Mos Eisley," Fennec said.

"I'll do the maintenance myself," Fett told her. "There's an advantage to people thinking you're dead." He sat back. "Now your debt is paid. Where would you like to be dropped?"

She looked at him from the corner of her eye. "Where are you headed?"

"I have a few scores to settle," Fett said.

Fennec thought about it for a long moment. "I'll go for the ride," she said.

SIXTEEN

TRACKING DOWN the Nikto speeder bike gang wasn't difficult. Fett already knew where they ran, and soaring above, he spotted them a long way off. He felt anger tightening his chest at the sight of the killers who had murdered the Tuskens. Dropping down, he opened fire on the gang, taking the last one out with a rocket that blew the bike and rider into oblivion. As the ship pulled out of attack position, Fett looked over at Fennec to gauge her response. She just nodded.

"Hang on," he said as they took off again, skimming through the sky over the desert toward their next destination.

"The Sarlacc pit," Fett said as the ship hovered above the gaping maw studded with daggerlike teeth. "That's where I was trapped all those years ago. That's where I'll find my armor."

"In there?" Fennec asked. "It's dissolved."

"Not beskar." He guided the ship downward into the mouth of the pit. Darkness engulfed the cockpit as they continued their slow descent, and he switched on his sensors. "I can't see a thing."

"Be careful," Fennec said.

Fett activated the exterior spotlights, shining them over the walls of the pit, where rings of teeth sprouted out all around them. He could see the wrinkled walls of the intestinal tract and layers of soft tissue, all of it motionless, waiting.

Then, suddenly, the thing leapt up at them, seizing hold of the Firespray with its muscular tentacles.

"Shoot it!" Fennec shouted.

Fett opened fire, but to no effect. The ship groaned as the Sarlacc began dragging it downward. Alarms wailed and blinked on the ship's display, and the Sarlacc roared at them hungrily, pulling harder.

Fennec unbuckled herself and reached up to tap a button on the console, releasing a seismic charge. The charge slid downward and landed in the maw of the Sarlacc, which swallowed it.

"Fire in the hole," Fennec said.

THH-OOOOMM!

The ground trembled with the seismic explosion, rippling outward from the pit. An instant later, the ship rose free, with the last severed tentacles of the Sarlacc sliding from its hull. Fennec sank back with a gasp of relief.

Fett kept his eyes on the pit below. "Next time," he said, "don't touch my buttons."

Later, with the Sarlacc dead, Boba Fett descended again into the Great Pit of Carkoon in search of his armor. When he returned, struggling for air and climbing up the rope, he saw Fennec waiting to find out what he'd found.

"Nothing," he gasped. "It's all junk."

"You're burning," she said. "It's not safe there." She began pouring water over his scalp, rinsing the corrosive digestive fluids from his skin.

"My armor's down there," Fett said.

"It served its purpose," she said. "It saved you from the acid." She handed him the bottle. "What you need to find is a bacta tank."

That night, Fett and Fennec sat outside the ship, sharing a dinner of flame-roasted scurrier as they discussed the future. "Are you serious about forming your own house?" she asked.

Fett answered her question with one of his own. "How many times have you been hired to do a job that was avoidable," he asked, "if they only took the time to think? How much money could've been made? How many lives could've been saved?"

"Then you and I would be out of work," Fennec said.

"I'm tired of our kind dying because of the idiocy of others," Fett said. "We're smarter than them. It's time we took our shot."

Fennec glanced at him. "We?"

"Yes," Fett said. "If I'm going to start a house, I need brains and muscle. You have both."

"It's tempting," she admitted. "But I'm an independent contractor. I'll do jobs for you, but I value my freedom."

"I can offer you something no client ever has," Fett said.

"What's that?"

"Loyalty. I will cut you in on the success, and pledge my life to protect yours."

"Living with the Tuskens has made you soft," Fennec said.

"No," Fett said. "It's made me strong." He peered up at her, his features flickering in the firelight, and shared the lesson he'd learned during his time among the Sand People. "You can only get so far without a tribe."

SEVENTEEN

"**CONGRATULATIONS,** Master Fett," 8D8 said, holding up a robe outside the bacta tank. "You are completely healed."

Boba Fett climbed out of the tank and got dressed.

"Anything from the mayor's majordomo? Is he cooperating?" Fett asked Fennec as she walked over.

"Oh, he's singing like a Yuzzum," Fennec said. "But still no sign of the mayor."

"My armor, quickly," Fett told 8D8.

"Relax," Fennec said. "The Mods are combing the streets of Mos Espa. If he's here, they will find him."

"I should still show my face in town," Fett said. "Power hates a vacuum."

Fett stepped into Garsa's Sanctuary and took off his helmet in time to see Krrsantan, the Wookiee, beating up an entire group of Trandoshans. Krrsantan grabbed an unlucky Trandoshan and hoisted him into the air.

"I think you've made your point," Garsa said with characteristic diplomacy as she made her way to what remained of the gambling area.

Krrsantan stopped in the midst of his destruction, listening.

Garsa continued, "Is it not beneath you to dismember this unfortunate Trandoshan?"

The Trandoshan, whimpering, clearly agreed.

"Thousands once cheered such a display," Garsa said, laying a gentle hand on the Wookiee's shoulder, "but those days have passed." The Wookiee growled, but she lowered her voice to a near whisper, as if taking him into her confidence. "In this more civilized place, in these more civilized times, what was once celebrated in the bloodlust of the arena is now seen as horror and cruelty."

Krrsantan seemed to relax, loosening his grip on the Trandoshan slightly.

"There, now," Garsa said, smiling, "isn't that better? And you've nothing left to prove." She patted him. "You are a champion. You are above such pettiness. Now"—she extended one finger, her voice becoming a little more stern—"you *have* run up quite a bar tab, Santo. So what say you release this customer and let these fine folks get back to their fun. And in return"—another familiar, confidential smile—"I will wipe your debt off the books."

Krrsantan growled softly and turned to look at her, as if weighing the merit of her proposal. Then he ripped the Trandoshan's arm off.

The crowd let out a loud gasp of shock and disbelief as the severed arm hit the floor with an audible thump. Garsa took an exasperated breath and walked away.

The Wookiee dropped a fistful of credits into the hand of the nearest hostess and made his way toward the entrance, where Fett was still standing, taking all this in. Krrsantan paused long enough to give Fett a snarl, then walked out the door.

Fett glanced at Garsa. "It was worth a shot."

She shrugged and rolled her eyes, then gestured to the band leader. "Hit it, Max."

"Hey, mate."

At the sound of the voice behind him, the Wookiee stopped walking. He recognized the voice, of course—it belonged to Boba Fett.

"Looks like you could use a job," Fett said.

Slowly, growling, Krrsantan turned to listen to his offer.

Inside Boba Fett's palace, Fett and Fennec hosted a banquet for the local crime bosses, all of whom sat around the table listening to what Fennec had to say.

"Jabba the Hutt once sat upon that throne," she said. "His reign ended in a ball of fire on the Dune Sea, and then Bib Fortuna took his place." She gazed at the faces looking back at her. "You were all once captains under the Hutt, but you quickly left the family when Fortuna claimed to be the heir. He was a terrible leader with no right to the throne. Oh, you each tried to take his place, but were thwarted by his guile and treachery."

She advanced to the end of the table, where Fett sat.

"It took this man, Boba Fett, to remove him," Fennec continued. "You all accrued wealth and riches under Jabba the Hutt. You can again, if you listen to Boba Fett."

She took her seat, letting all this sink in, and Fett spoke up. "I may sit on that throne," he said. "But I have no designs on any of your territories. I ask for no tribute or quarter, and I expect to give none, either. I'm here to make a proposal that's mutually beneficial."

The listeners leaned in as he got to the heart of the matter.

"As I'm sure you all know," Fett continued, "the Pyke Syndicate are mustering troops in Mos Espa. They have slowly absorbed our planet as part of their spice trade. They have bribed the mayor and are draining Tatooine of its wealth."

"We make many credits from the sale of spice in our territories," said Dokk Strassi, on the opposite side of the table. He was the Trandoshan who had come to pay tribute to Fett earlier, and his smooth demeanor remained as cunning and untrustworthy as ever.

"Why do you deserve to be the daimyo?" a Klatooinian captain cut in with a snarl. "What prevents us all from killing you and taking what we want?"

All heads turned toward Fett, awaiting his response. But before he could say anything, a thunderous roar shook the floor, rattling the table and plates, jostling everyone out of their seats. The claws of the rancor burst up through the grate beneath them, and the captains all stared at each other as they backed away uneasily.

"Easy, boy," Fett said calmly as he dropped a chunk of meat down through the grate. "Easy. He is a little hungry." Looking up at the others, he gestured them back to the table. "Please, sit."

Cautiously, the captains returned to their chairs, and Fett continued.

"Why speak of conflict," he said, "when cooperation can make us all rich?"

An Aqualish captain spoke up in his own language, and 8D8 hastened to translate. "Master Garfalaquox asks what it is you are proposing."

"I am proposing that all the families of Mos Espa join in a defensive alliance until the Pyke Syndicate is vanquished," Fett said.

"They have only challenged *your* territory," the Klatooinian captain protested, jabbing one finger toward Fett for emphasis. "Why should we spill the blood of our ranks for a feud waged between you and the Pykes?"

Fett placed his hands on the table and rose to his feet. "Then I will fight these battles alone," he said. "I will vanquish these interlopers who threaten our planet. I will make the streets safe again so all in this room can prosper." He stared steadily back at them. "All I ask in return is that you remain neutral if the Pyke Syndicate approaches you to betray me."

The captains murmured to one another in their own languages, conferring.

"This will be acceptable," Strassi said, and the others agreed, raising their glasses.

"Do you trust them?" Fennec asked later that evening as she and Fett stood out on the balcony, watching their guests depart.

"I trust them to act in their own self-interest," Fett said. "My deal is a lot better than what the Syndicate would offer." He looked down at the lights of the captains' hover vehicles as they streaked away from the palace into the night. "They may be stubborn, but they are not foolish enough to not see that the Pykes would eventually take over the whole planet." He drew in a breath and let it out. "Either way, we must prepare for war."

"How much treasure do we have in reserve?" Fennec asked.

"I have plenty of credits," Fett said. "What I'm short on is muscle."

"Credits can buy muscle," Fennec told him. "If you know where to look."

Fett looked over at her, wondering if she had anyone in particular in mind. He had a very strong feeling that she did.

RETURN OF THE MANDALORIAN

EIGHTEEN

THE AIR INSIDE the slaughterhouse reeked of blood. The murmuring voices of Klatooinian butchers echoed off the tile walls as they worked, chopping and sawing. Workers pushed carts of uncooked meat across the damp floor. Others stood sharpening their cleavers or polishing their knives. Large chunks of animal carcass dangled on hooks from the ceiling.

One of the butchers glanced up as the figure stepped through the doorway. It was unusual to see visitors there, particularly ones in beskar armor.

The Mandalorian had arrived.

The bounty hunter walked past the slabs of meat, making his way toward the makeshift office on the far side of the room. Inside a Klatooinian sat behind a desk piled with credits. He was dressed slightly better than the butchers, in a brown vest and shirtsleeves, and he glared at the Mandalorian with undisguised distrust.

There were two others next to him, one seated, one standing, and Mando heard the footsteps of more workers who had followed him inside.

"You look lost," the Klatooinian behind the desk said.

"I'm here for Kaba Baiz," Mando said.

"What makes you think he's here?"

Mando pulled out a tracking beacon and showed it to him, the red light blinking steadily.

"What do you want of him?" the Klatooinian demanded.

"He owes someone important money."

"Who?"

"That's not my business," Mando said. "I'm here to bring him in."

"Well, if I see him, I'll let him know."

Mando took out a holopuck and activated it, placing it on the desk. "I see him right now," he said.

"That's not me." The Klatooinian chuckled at the image in the hologram, glancing at one of the henchmen next to him. "That doesn't even look like me."

Mando turned to acknowledge the presence of the half dozen or so thugs that were standing around him. "I'm going to give the rest of you the opportunity to walk out that door," he said. "I have no quarrel with you."

Baiz sat back, shaking his head. "They're not going anywhere," he said. "Looks to me like you're surrounded. But you look like the practical type." He gestured to the desk full of coins. "Let's discuss our options."

Mando didn't answer for a moment. "I can bring you in warm," he said, unsnapping his blaster holster, "or I can bring you in cold."

Out of nowhere, one of the thugs lunged forward and bit Mando's hand, forcing him to drop the blaster. Mando headbutted him, spun around, and drove his knee up into the chest of another of Baiz's enforcers. Behind him, one of them opened fire with a blaster, the bolts deflecting off Mando's beskar.

Mando reached down and unsheathed the Darksaber. Its black blade crackled as he swung it down, chopping off one of the assailant's hands at the wrist. When two more attacked him, Mando dispatched them with an elbow strike and a kick to the face. He swung the Darksaber again, but its weight had begun dragging against the floor. Hoisting it up, Mando hacked through a chunk of hanging meat, then raised the saber higher and lunged, thrusting it forward to impale another of the thugs through the stomach.

As Mando pulled the blade back, he felt a sudden blaze of agony in his leg. Glancing down, he saw that he'd cut himself with the Darksaber. Gritting his teeth, he managed to fight off the last two assailants, knocking them out. Blaster fire was ricocheting off his back, and he realized that Baiz had come out from behind the desk and was shooting at him.

Mando spun around and charged him, stabbing him in the chest with a vibroblade and slamming Baiz's body down on top of the desk. Then with a grunt of effort, he raised the Darksaber high over his head and brought it down, cleaving the Klatooinian completely in half along with the desk. Both Baiz and the desk collapsed, smashing to the floor.

When Mando emerged from the office, the other workers were gathered outside staring at him, wide-eyed.

"Your boss is dead," Mando said. "I'm here to collect on his bounty." He indicated the bag in his hand containing Baiz's severed head. "I have no trouble with any of you. There's a pile of New Republic credits in there that I have no right to. If you do me the honor of letting me pass, you all can help yourselves to whatever you think you deserve from your former employer."

Exchanging uncertain glances with his coworkers, one of the butchers began to creep past Mando, then the rest poured into the office. When they had all gone in, Mando began to limp slowly out of the room.

Boba Fett, wounded and exhausted, escapes the Sarlacc pit.

Fett is captured by Tusken Raiders, who eventually welcome him into their tribe.

Boba Fett shows his tribe a new way to fight back against the criminal Pyke Syndicate.

The Pykes destroy the Tusken tribe but make Fett think a Nikto gang is responsible.

Boba Fett teams up with assassin Fennec Shand to retrieve his ship from Jabba the Hutt's palace.

Together, Fett and Fennec succeed in taking over Jabba's throne.

The Hutt twins say that Jabba's former territory belongs to them, but Boba Fett disagrees.

After failing to defeat Boba Fett, the Twins present him with a young rancor as a gift.

Garsa Fwip, owner of the Sanctuary, angers the Pyke Syndicate by cooperating with Boba Fett.

Meanwhile, fellow Mandalorian Paz Vizsla challenges Mando to a fight for the Darksaber.

Peli Motto restores a Naboo starfighter to replace Mando's ship, the *Razor Crest*.

The Mandalorian tries to visit Grogu, but former Jedi Ahsoka Tano tells him to leave for Grogu's sake.

Grogu's mind is not on his Jedi training.

Luke Skywalker tells Grogu to choose: return to the Mandalorian or train to become a Jedi.

Cad Bane is a lethal bounty hunter who works for the Pykes.

Boba Fett asks Mando to stand with him and Fennec against the Pyke Syndicate.

Boba Fett enlists the help of the Mods, a Mos Espa grav scoot gang.

The Pykes launch their attack! Boba Fett and the Mandalorian battle side by side.

The former gladiator Wookiee Krrsantan fights for Boba Fett and his allies.

Grogu arrives wearing the beskar armor Mando had made for him. The clan of two is reunited.

Boba Fett battles the Scorpenek droids while riding on the back of the rancor!

After the rancor's rampage, Grogu uses the Force to put the creature to sleep.

Boba Fett defeats Cad Bane and secures peace for his territory.

The ring-shaped megastructure of Glavis was a constantly shifting cityscape of light and dark, its architecture illuminated by perpetual cycles of obstructed and unobstructed starlight. Mando walked along the artificial gravity of its streets with the bagged head in his hand and made his way toward the turbolift of the tower that stood before him.

As the lift rose, he felt the eyes of a curious Caskadag fix on the bag. Mando glanced at the Caskadag, who quickly looked away.

The lift halted, opening onto a large club-like space with atmospheric music playing softly overhead and people dancing and mingling casually in the background. Mando walked over to a table by the wall, where a green-skinned Ishi Tib sat with her entourage, enjoying her meal. "That was fast," she said, speaking in Huttese. She had large eyes that protruded from stalks on either side of her head, and a beak-like mouth twisting into what might've been a smile, or a sneer. "You're a good hunter."

Mando put the bagged head on the table in front of him. "I'd like my reward and the information you promised."

"Why are you rushing business, Mando?"

"My business is my own," he said. "Where is it?"

The Ishi Tib didn't bother to hide her disappointment. "Sit and enjoy a meal with us."

"Where is the closest access to the substrata?"

"Sit and feast with us," his prospective hostess said petulantly, "or I will tell you nothing."

"You can keep your reward," Mando said. "There's a bounty on this Klatooinian." He picked up the head. "If you don't give me the information, someone else will."

"It's down Kolzoc Alley by the heat vent towers," she said. "Please sit. I have another job for you."

Mando dropped the head back on the table. "I'd put that on ice if I were you," he advised, and turned to go back to the turbolift.

By the time he'd descended to the substrata, the pain from the self-inflicted Darksaber burn on his leg had become even more intense. Worse, the leg itself felt badly weakened and untrustworthy, and he almost fell off the ladder leading into the lower depths of the city.

Activating the multispectral scanner in his helmet, Mando studied the hidden mythosaur symbols on the wall, directing him forward. Following the trail, he entered a hatch leading down a concealed stairwell.

Mando took one step at a time, clutching the railing to keep himself upright. Ahead of him he could see a figure seated at the end of a long walkway overlooking the starry expanse beyond the city's looping ring. He reached the bottom step, and his leg gave out completely, sending him to the floor with a clatter.

Slowly, the figure at the end of the walkway looked around.

"Tend to him," the Armorer said.

Mando lifted his head and saw his fellow Mandalorian Paz Vizsla approaching with a medical kit. "I didn't know if I would ever see you again," Paz said as he examined the burn on Mando's leg.

"Thank you for saving me on Nevarro," Mando said. "I am sorry for your sacrifice."

"There are three of us now," Paz said. He began to apply bacta spray to Mando's leg wound while Mando groaned in pain. "We'll put you to work soon enough."

"What weapon caused such a wound?" the Armorer inquired.

Mando reached down and held up the Darksaber. "This."

"Paz Vizsla, bring it to me."

Paz took the Darksaber from Mando's hand, studying it as he walked it over to where the Armorer was waiting.

"All this talk of the Empire," she said, taking the weapon, "and they lasted less than thirty years. Mandalorians have existed for ten thousand." She switched on the Darksaber, holding it aloft. "What do you know of this blade?"

"I am told it is the Darksaber," Mando said.

"Indeed. Do you understand its significance?"

"Whoever wields it can lead all of Mandalore."

"If it is won by Creed in battle," the Armorer told him, holding the black blade in front of her face. "It is said, one warrior will defeat twenty, and the multitudes will fall before it. If, however, it is not won in combat and falls into the hands of the undeserving, it will be a curse unto the nations." She deactivated the blade. "Mandalore will be laid to waste and its people scattered to the four winds."

Grunting, Mando got to his feet and looked at her. "The hilt is of a quality of beskar I have never seen before."

"It was forged over a thousand years ago by the

Mandalore Tarre Vizsla," the Armorer said. "He was both Mandalorian and Jedi."

"I have met Jedi," Mando said.

"Then you have completed your quest," she said. "And you may join our covert as we rebuild."

Mando nodded. "This is the Way."

"This is the Way," echoed Paz Vizsla.

The Armorer extended her hand, returning the Darksaber to Mando. "This is the Way."

NINETEEN

REBUILDING THE COVERT was hard work and required all Mando's strength, especially while he was still recovering from the wound on his leg. As he and Paz Vizsla hoisted the smelter into place, assembling its various components, Paz glanced up at him speculatively.

"Where did you come upon the Darksaber?" he asked.

"I defeated Moff Gideon," Mando said.

"Did you kill him?"

"No," Mando said, "but he was sent off to the New Republic for interrogation, and he will face justice for his crimes."

Paz grunted. "Death would've been justice for his atrocities."

"This is true," the Armorer said as she entered. "The blood of millions of our kind is on his hands."

"Then he will be executed for his crimes by the New Republic tribunal," Mando said.

"We shall see." She activated the smelter, sending up a cloud of steam from the cauldron. "The songs of eons past foretold of the mythosaur rising up to herald a new age of Mandalore." She opened the wall console in front of her and took out the smelting tools. "Sadly, it only exists in legends. Where did you come upon the beskar spear?"

Mando reached back, withdrawing the spear from where it hung over his shoulder. "It was the gift of a Jedi. It can block a lightsaber. I used it to defeat Moff Gideon."

"It can also pierce beskar armor," the Armorer said. "Its mere existence puts Mandalorians at risk. Mandalorian steel is meant for armor, not weapons."

Mando held the spear out to her. "Then forge it into armor."

She took it from him. "The Darksaber is a more noble weapon for you to wield," she said, and placed the spear on the edge of the smelter.

Mando sat down on the other side of the chamber and looked up at her. "Have you ever heard of Bo-Katan Kryze?"

"Bo-Katan is a cautionary tale," the Armorer said

as she poured liquid from a tube into the container. "She once laid claim to rule Mandalore based purely on blood, and the sword you now possess. But it was gifted to her and not won by Creed. Bo-Katan Kryze was born of a mighty house, but they lost sight of the Way."

Placing the tip of the spear in the smelter's blue jets of flame, she heated it until it glowed red-hot.

"Her rule ended in tragedy," she continued. "They lost their way, and we lost our world. Had our sect not been cloistered on the moon of Concordia, we would have not survived the Great Purge. Eventually, Imperial interlopers destroyed all that we knew and loved in the Night of a Thousand Tears."

Mando listened as the Armorer's words evoked a litany of terrible images in his mind. He could all too easily imagine TIE bombers strafing Mandalore with weapons of mass destruction. First the bombers had assaulted Sundari, destroying it in a vast, all-consuming firestorm of boiling smoke and flame. Afterward, Viper probe droids and KX security droids scoured the ruins for survivors, executing them with brutal efficiency.

"Only those that walked the Way escaped the curse prophesied in the Creed," the Armorer continued. "Though our numbers were scattered to the winds, our adherence to the Way has preserved our legacy for the generations until we may someday return to our home-world." She raised the spear, studying its glowing tip. "What shall I forge?"

"Something for a foundling," Mando said.

"This is the Way."

"For a specific foundling," he said. "Grogu."

She looked up at him. "He is no longer in your care. He is with his own kind now."

"I want to see him," Mando said, "make sure he's safe."

"In order to master the ways of the Force," the Armorer said, "Jedi must forgo all attachment."

"That is the opposite of our Creed," Mando said. "Loyalty and solidarity are the way."

"What shall I forge for the foundling Grogu?"

Mando told her and waited while she worked, hammering the heated beskar and forging the results into small links of chain mail. When it was finished, she wrapped the item in a piece of cloth and handed it to him.

"Solus," the Armorer called out, counting in Mando'a, *"t'ad, ehn, cuir."*

She and Mando were up on a scaffolding, practicing sword fighting. Mando wielded the Darksaber while the Armorer attacked, using her tools against the blade with a series of crashes and clangs. With every swing, Mando felt the Darksaber growing more unwieldy in his grasp, and soon he was grunting and struggling to maintain equilibrium simply holding it up. When he took one last swing, the momentum knocked him off balance and he staggered over the edge.

"You are fighting against the blade," she said as Mando used his jet pack to fly back into position.

"It gets heavier with each move," he said, barely able to rise above a kneeling position.

"That is because you are fighting against the blade," she repeated. "You *should* be fighting against your opponent. Stand up."

Groaning with effort, Mando forced himself to his feet. The Darksaber was so heavy in his grasp that he had to drag it across the metal latticework under his feet, hardly able to raise the tip. Just as he'd managed to get the blade up to eye level, the Armorer went at him with a quick series of blows from her tools, hammering him backward and forcing him into submission.

"There," she said. "Feel it? You are too weak to fight the Darksaber." She pressed down. "It will win if you fight against it. You cannot control it with your strength."

Mando stood up, catching his breath. "I want to try again."

"Persistence without insight will lead to the same outcome," she said firmly. "Your body is strong, but your mind is distracted."

"I am focused."

"The blade says otherwise."

From the other end of the platform, Paz Vizsla emerged into view. "Maybe the Darksaber belongs in someone else's hands," he said.

Mando gazed at him. "Maybe."

"It was forged by my ancestor, founder of House Vizsla."

"And now it belongs to me," Mando said.

"Because you won it in combat."

"That's right."

"And now I will win it from you," Paz said, striding toward him.

The Armorer turned to Mando. "Do you agree to this duel, Din Djarin?"

"I do," Mando said.

She walked away and left the two standing face to face, squaring off on either end of the platform. Mando and Paz both removed their jet packs, setting them aside. Mando switched on the Darksaber, immediately aware of its weight in his hands. Paz activated his gauntlet shield and drew his vibroblade, and Mando went at him.

He swung the saber, and Paz deflected it with his shield. They exchanged a quick series of blows, and Mando could already feel the Darksaber's power straining against his muscles as Paz headbutted him with his helmet and flung Mando backward. Paz grabbed Mando's shoulders and rammed his head into a stanchion, then bent down to pick up the fallen Darksaber.

"Fate has brought this blade back to my clan," Paz growled as he swung the saber, "and now fate will end yours."

Mando ducked, and the Darksaber's blade hissed past him, colliding with the wall in a spray of sparks. Paz was struggling to pry it loose, laboring to free it from where it was stuck—he'd dropped his guard. Mando slammed Paz in the chest, driving the air from his lungs, then grabbed his vibroblade and put it to Paz's throat, holding him there.

"It is done," the Armorer said, ending the duel. "Paz Vizsla, have you ever removed your helmet?"

"No," Paz said.

"Has it ever been removed by others?"

"Never."

"This is the Way."

"This is the Way," Paz repeated.

"Din Djarin, have you ever removed your helmet?"

Mando remained motionless, saying nothing, holding the blade in place against Paz's neck, and the Armorer asked again.

"Have you ever removed your helmet?" She waited. "By Creed, you must vow."

Mando lowered the vibroblade and released Paz, shoving him aside and standing up. "I have."

"Then you are a Mandalorian no more," the Armorer said.

Mando felt his chest tighten at this pronouncement. The Armorer's declaration hung over him like a death sentence. "I beg you for your forgiveness," he said. "How can I atone?"

"Leave, apostate," Paz snarled from the floor beneath him.

"According to Creed," the Armorer said, "one may only be redeemed in the living waters beneath the mines of Mandalore."

"But the mines have all been destroyed," Mando said.

"This is the Way," she said.

Mando bent down to pick up the Darksaber. There was nothing more to say. He walked away from Paz Vizsla, past the Armorer, and out of the covert, heading to the surface of the ring city.

TWENTY

FLYING COMMERCIAL was not Mando's first preference, but with no ship to his name, he didn't have a choice. Flight 1020 was a nonstop spaceliner to Tatooine, and as he approached the gangplank, a security alarm went off.

"Excuse me, sir," the RX-series droid said. "You're going to have to remove your weapons."

"I'm a Mandalorian," Mando said. "Weapons are part of my religion."

"I'm sorry, sir. You can't board a commercial flight with your weapons. If you wish to discuss this with my supervisor, I will gladly book you on tomorrow's flight."

Mando sighed. "Fine," he said. As the other passengers streamed past him, he took out his blaster pistol and whistling birds, then added the pliers and flamethrower, the shells from his bandolier, his grappling cable, his vibroblade, and finally the Darksaber, placing them all inside a cargo container and locking it. He pointed up at the droid. "I know everything that's in there."

"Proceed," the droid said.

Mando turned to board the liner.

After liftoff, he reclined in the passenger lounge, staring out at the stars. He had the sense of being watched, and looked over to see a young Rodian in front of him, eyeing Mando over the seat. The child waved, and one of his parents told him to sit down. Mando glanced down at the cloth bundle containing the beskar chain mail he'd asked the Armorer to forge for Grogu.

The starliner flew onward.

Mando arrived in Mos Eisley spaceport and retrieved his weapons, then made his way to hangar three-five. He was hoping to find Peli Motto, but he wasn't expecting to find her in the process of being dragged away by a womp rat.

"It's got me!" she was shrieking to her droids as the rat pulled her behind a crate of equipment. "It's chewing! Help!"

TCHHAOOW! From behind her, Mando fired a single round and blasted the rat off Peli's leg.

"What an entrance," Peli said, standing up to check on the droids that had been cowering in fear during the attack. "Hey, look, everyone. Mando's back!"

The droids stalked off with mournful groans.

"What do we owe the pleasure?" Peli asked as they walked out of the hangar. "You here to slay another dragon? Chasing down some elusive bounty?"

"I got your message," Mando said. "You said you found me a replacement for the *Razor Crest*."

"Yeah," Peli said, "that's right. That's what I said. That's what I do. I've been working my butt off, yeah." She eyed him hopefully. "Did you bring the cash?"

"It's right here," Mando said, handing it over.

"Mind if I count it? Not that I don't trust you. I just wanna make sure you don't give me too much." Peli looked over at the droids. "Hey, make yourselves useful. Count this up, and then fire up the grill before that womp rat gets gamy." She turned to Mando. "Right this way. Wait till you get your eyes on this baby." As they walked, she asked him, "So, where's your unlikely companion?"

"I returned him to his own kind," Mando said.

"Why would you do that?" Peli asked, and chuckled. "I could've made good money off that thing. Open a petting zoo."

"Where's the ship?"

"Right this way." She led him into another berth, where a tarp covered a large object in the middle of the open space. "Ready to have your mind blown?"

With a dramatic gesture, she pulled away the cover to reveal the skeleton of a stripped-down starfighter. Mando stared at it for a moment in confusion. Entire sheets of the fighter's cowling were missing, exposing the internal electronics of the vessel, none of which appeared to be in good repair.

"Where's the Razor Crest?" he asked.

"I never said I had a Razor Crest. I said I had a replacement for a Razor Crest."

Mando shook his head. "I don't have time for this."

"Hang on a second," Peli said. "Do you have any idea what this is? This is an N-1 starfighter, handmade for the royal guard and commissioned personally by the queen of Naboo."

"This," Mando said, pointing, "is a pile of junk."

Peli sighed. "Do you want your credits back?"

"Yes."

"No skin off my dip-swap," she said, and shouted

for her pit droids. "Droids, bring this lovely man his money!" She looked at Mando again. "Here you go. It's that easy. Sorry to waste your time. Okay?" She sighed again, crossed her arms, and rocked back on her heels, gazing at the partially disassembled starfighter. "While we're waiting, can I at least tell you a little something about this honey? I know she doesn't look like much, but you got here a lot earlier than I expected, and I didn't get a chance to finish. I mean, clearly, you can see, I've got all the parts right here."

A piece fell off the starfighter and landed on the floor with a clang.

"Do you know how hard it is to find all original parts from way back in the Galactic Republic?" Peli asked. "I mean, these are all handmade. *No droids*. And not only that, what I'm gonna do, just because I like you, is I'm gonna add on some custom modification that'll make her faster than a fathier, and because this baby's pre-Empire, she's off the grid." She glanced up hopefully at Mando, her sales pitch gathering steam. "And did I mention, she can jump into hyperspace with no docking ring? I mean, come on! You gotta see the potential."

Mando leaned down and tugged on a piece of the cooling manifold, which snapped off, splashing liquid on the floor.

"I'm telling you, Mando," Peli said, "you gotta believe me. This is a classic. At least let me put her together for you before you decide. Will you give me that? Mm? There you go."

Mando didn't say anything as Peli grabbed a handful of tools.

"Let's get this baby up and going," she said. "You know, it'd be a lot faster if you helped."

She handed him a wrench.

Later, Mando was working underneath the starfighter as Peli's BD droid flashed a light on the undercarriage of the ship. It was slow going because the droid kept moving its head when Mando needed to see what he was doing. "Just focus right here," he said, pointing. "Just stop moving and aim it right here."

"Great news," Peli said, pushing a cart with a circular piece of equipment on it. "I found you a turbonic venturi power assimilator! You're gonna be the fastest ship on the Outer Rim."

Mando slid out from underneath the fighter and walked over to inspect the assimilator. "Where did you get this?"

"It's brand-new," Peli said proudly. "Well, *Jawa* new."

"The Jawas had a turbonic venturi assimilator from a Galactic Republic-era starfighter?"

"Well, they didn't have it. They *got* it."

"From where?"

"Tatooine is a garden of many bounties," Peli said.

Mando just looked at her. "I don't understand."

"I gave 'em a list of parts, and they found them for me," she said. "I don't ask, they don't tell. They give me what I ask for. In exchange, I let 'em pick through my dumpster."

"Can I meet them?" Mando asked.

"Yeah, sure." She raised her voice. "Arfive! See if the Jawas are still out back!" As R5-D4 rolled away, Peli turned back to Mando and continued in a quieter voice: "Dated a Jawa for a while. They're quite furry. Very furry. Lotta issues . . ."

Behind her, a pair of Jawas approached, chattering with each other, eyes gleaming beneath their hoods.

"Oh, here they are," Peli said.

"If I give them a list of parts," Mando said, "could they get them for me?"

Peli turned, speaking in Jawaese, and the three spent a moment parlaying back and forth. "They said make a wish list," Peli said, "and they'll see what's available."

"Okay," Mando said. "I'm looking for mostly bolt-on aftermarket speed mods. This is all hand-built, custom. I'm guessing we need vintage hyperware if it's gonna fit this antique."

"Listen to you," Peli said. "Don't worry about the shape and size. Just get the parts you want with the specs you need, and I'm gonna make it work, all right?" She smiled. "I told you that I dated a Jawa. I know what I'm doing, right?"

One of the Jawas responded to her enthusiastically.

"Oh, that's all right," Peli said. "I'm working on me right now. Just go find the parts." Then she glanced at Mando. "Furry," she murmured.

TWENTY-ONE

MANDO AND PELI worked side by side rebuilding the starfighter, a process that, among other things, involved all her droids scouring parts from the scrap heap around the hangar, assembling them, and handing them to her. The longer they spent on it, the more Mando began to wonder if any of this was actually going to function properly in the sky—if he even managed to get it in the sky at all.

"The entire vapor manifold is missing," he told Peli.

"Trust me," she said from inside the cockpit, "the last thing you want strangling your thrust capacitor is a vapor manifold. I fabricated this induction intake charger that's gonna double your output coefficient."

"It'll also blow the shaft out of my motivator block," Mando said.

"That's why I'm reinforcing your compression housing," Peli said, "and you can access it by using this Kineso-switch right here." She pointed at the red switch inside the hatch. "You hit this button, you're really gonna evacuate your exhaust manifold, if you know what I mean."

Later, she used a power droid to charge up the ship's drive while Mando held up a curved piece of the engine cowling. "Where does this panel go?" The BD used its hologram projector to demonstrate where the panel fit. "Thanks, little guy."

"Do you know how lucky you are that I got my hands on this baby?" Peli asked as they fit the manifold into place. "You wanna thank me now, or you wanna thank me later?"

"You get me a Razor Crest," Mando said, "you can have it right back."

"Oh, bantha diddle," Peli said. "These are a lot harder to come by than some plain old Razor Crest." As she and Mando worked with the droids to cover the N-1's hull, Mando saw the two Jawas from earlier returning to the hangar carrying a long cylindrical structure on their shoulders.

"That was fast," he said.

"These critters could find a skud in a krill pond," Peli said, clearly pleased with his reaction. "Will that do?"

Mando picked up the part, inspecting it. "Where did they get a cryogenic density combustion booster?"

"Do you *really* want to know?" Peli asked.

"Sure."

She turned and spoke to the Jawas, who answered in a lively burst of narrative.

A moment later, Peli turned to Mando. "They said they crawled under a Pyke spice runner and crimped it off while they were refueling."

Mando regarded the Jawas with newfound respect. "Gutsy little fellas."

"Let me tell you something," Peli said, "Pykes do not mess around. Ever since they've been moving spice through the system, everything's a mess. Everyone's afraid of 'em, and law enforcement won't even go near 'em."

"Well, thanks," Mando said, tossing a sack of credits to the Jawas.

"Thanks?" Peli said, shocked, as the Jawas scurried away, gloating over their newfound fortune. "What? Are you kidding me? What'd you do that for? You're gonna spoil 'em! Are you trying to make me look bad?"

After Peli's droids finally pushed the fighter out of the hangar and into the daylight, she and Mando circled the ship, admiring their handiwork. "Not a gram of fat on her," Peli declared, using her sleeve to buff the gleaming wing. "You know, no one's catching you in this thing."

Mando reached the back of the fighter. "What happened to the droid port?"

"I hogged it out," Peli said. "You know, I figured with your disposition, you'd want to forgo the astromech."

Mando bent down, turning his head to look alongside the lines of the fighter, inspecting the wings and hull. "You think she's ready?"

"Ready as she'll ever be," Peli said. "Start her up."

"Really?"

"Yeah, start her up."

Mando climbed in the cockpit. The engine sputtered and died. "It's not turning over," he said.

"Give it a little bit more juice."

Beep! He flicked the switch on the power igniter, and this time the engines jumped to life powerfully enough to make the whole starfighter tremble and shake. "That's a lot of engine for a little ship," he shouted over the roar of the turbines.

"Yeah, well, see what she can do," Peli said.

"Shouldn't we run a diagnostic first?"

"Nah!" Peli yelled back. "I can hear her! She's purring! Send her up!"

Mando closed the cockpit and brought the fighter up into the air. "Engaging forward drives," he said, and took off, skimming over the city below. "She handles a little bumpy."

"You're used to a gunship." Peli's voice came through the earpiece. "But she's a starfighter, so fly her like one."

"Okay," Mando said, "I'll open her up." He hit the throttle and felt the ship respond immediately, blazing across the outskirts of Mos Eisley and into the open desert, heading for the rock formations outside the city. "*Dank farrik*, she's fast."

"Smooth?" Peli asked.

"As a gonk's scomp jack," Mando said.

"There you go!" Peli exclaimed with laughter. "Some teamwork."

"Controls are real snappy," he said. "How's the maneuverability?"

"You tell me," Peli said. "Point your navigational disposition between the two suns. You'll come up to Beggar's Canyon."

Mando angled the ship sideways and skimmed through a narrow gap between two rock formations.

"How's the handling?" Peli asked.

"Tight," Mando said. "She tracks like a railspeeder." Cutting through Beggar's Canyon, he startled a womp rat and sent it scurrying into the shadows, then pulled back on the yoke, angling the fighter up. "Let's see what she's got."

The N-1 shot skyward, tearing across Tatooine's outer atmosphere and into space. Gaining elevation, Mando caught sight of a commercial starliner and drew up alongside it. Looking over, he saw the young Rodian from earlier inside, peering out at him. Mando gave him a nod, hit the thrusters, and shot off, taking the fighter through a series of acrobatic spins.

A second later there was an electronic chirp as the N-1's proximity sensors alerted him to nearby traffic.

"*Dank farrik*," Mando muttered, and glanced over at the two New Republic X-wings coming up to flank him on either side.

"Run your beacon for me, N-1," one of the pilot's said, voice crackling.

"Was I doing something wrong, Officer?" Mando asked.

"You're not allowed to fly that fast next to a commercial ship," the New Republic pilot informed him.

"You're also operating without a beacon. I'm gonna need you to run one for us."

"Sorry, Officer," Mando said. "I got a little carried away there. Transmitting now."

There was radio silence while the pilot consulted the incoming beacon information. "Hm," he said. "Your engine model doesn't match your power drive."

"We just built her," Mando said. "I was taking her up for a test flight. Haven't been able to update the registration just yet."

"We're gonna need to see your title tabs. Send us a ping."

"Yeah, sorry, Officer," Mando said, "but my transmitter isn't hooked up yet. I'll head right back to Mos Eisley and get it sorted out."

The X-wing pilot's response was terse and authoritative. "Relinquish your flight controls for remote-control access."

"Hold on a second, there, Lieutenant," the second, older pilot said, speaking for the first time. "I think we can let him off with a warning this time."

"Thank you, Officer," Mando said. "I'll have that taken care of."

"One thing before you go," the second pilot said.

"Your voice is mighty familiar. Did you used to fly a Razor Crest?"

"I think you have the wrong guy, Officer."

"That ship showed up on a transponder log back in Nevarro in an incident involving Imperial remnants," the older pilot said. "I'm just connecting some dots here. You mind answering a few questions?"

Mando hovered in position for a moment, glanced over at the other pilot, then reached down and hit his thrusters. The N-1 streaked away, leaving the two X-wings behind, the pilots startled by its sudden departure.

"How did it jump?" the first pilot asked. "He didn't power up his hyperdrives!"

"Didn't jump, kid," the older pilot said. "Those were sublight thrusters."

"There's no trace of him on our sensors. Are we reporting this?"

"You want to go back to base, fill out reports all day?"

The younger pilot chuckled. "No, sir," he said.

The two X-wings peeled away and headed off in the opposite direction.

"Well?" Peli said when Mando landed. "How was it?"

Mando opened the canopy. "Wizard."

"Those J-type pulse engines really tighten the old evacuation port, don't they?"

Mando climbed down from the cockpit and started walking across the hangar.

"Oh, by the way," Peli said, "an old friend of yours dropped by. Said she was looking for you."

Mando stopped and looked around. "A friend of mine?"

"Don't worry. I told her I didn't know where you were. Then I locked her out and engaged the hangar security system."

"She tell you her name?"

"Fennec Shand," someone said overhead. Peli shrieked in surprise, and Mando looked up to see Fennec perched on a ventilation pipe sticking out of the hangar wall.

"I thought you said that the hangar security system was on," Peli snapped at her droids as Fennec leapt down to the ground and walked over to Mando.

"By any chance are you looking for work?" she asked.

"I could be," Mando said.

She brought out a sack of coins and tossed it over. "Pay is good."

"What's the bounty?"

"No bounty," Fennec said. "We need muscle."

Mando understood why she'd come. "Boba Fett," he said.

"He sure would appreciate it."

Mando weighed the sack of credits for a moment, then tossed it back to her. "Tell him it's on the house," he said. "But first I've got to pay a visit to a little friend."

FROM THE DESERT COMES A STRANGER

TWENTY-TWO

THE MIDDAY SUNS beat down on the desert outskirts of Mos Pelgo as a group of Pyke couriers gathered next to a moisture vaporator. One of them placed the chest of spice on top of their landspeeder while another produced the payment to complete the transaction.

"It's all there," the first courier said.

"We'll leave the spice," the second one replied, "and take the credits back to Mos Eisley. The rest will follow—"

"Do you know where you are, gentlemen?" someone behind them asked.

The Pykes spun around, one of them already reaching for his blaster.

"Think it through," Marshal Cobb Vanth said calmly. His hand was already resting on the handle of his blaster. "I'll give you the benefit of the doubt, being you're not from around here, and say you figured you're in the middle of nowhere. But everything out there"—squinting, he pointed to the desert beyond them—"is the Mos Pelgo territories." He tapped the markings on the front of his gun belt. "And these stripes indicate I'm the marshal of said territories. Now, I don't know what arrangements you have with the authorities of Mos Espa, and let's be honest, in Mos Eisley, anything goes. But out here, I'm the one who tells folks what to do."

The Pykes glowered at him in uneasy silence.

"I didn't see what's in that chest," Vanth continued, his tone still reasonable, "and consequently, no laws have been broken, as far as I'm concerned. If you gentlemen load up your wares and head back to where you came, we can chalk this one up to you guys reading the map wrong."

One of the Pykes turned slowly to the courier next to him as if to confer with him, then spun around, blaster in hand. It was a bad decision, and it would be his last.

KSHHEWW! SHEWW-SHEWW! Before they could even fire, three of the four Pykes lay dead on the ground, and the marshal pointed his pistol at the fourth. "Think it through," he said again.

The remaining courier raised his hands in the air. Slowly, Vanth walked toward him.

"I can see you're the smart one," he said. "I got a proposition for your bosses. Tell 'em I've heard of the Syndicate. Take their credits back with you. And I say this with respect: anyone who gets lost running spice through Mos Pelgo again will be lost forever."

The courier didn't respond.

"Now unload that chest and go," Vanth said. "Consider it a fine for trespassing."

"It's worth more than your town," the Pyke growled.

The marshal eyed him mildly. "Well, then, maybe I'll retire."

The Pyke placed the chest of spice on the ground, returned the container of credits, and prepared to leave. Vanth twirled his pistol back into its holster and watched the speeder move away. When it was gone, he sauntered over to the bodies of the dead Pykes, where the chest sat, and used the toe of his boot to flip open the lid. The spice within it was orangey-brown and fine but otherwise unremarkable, not so different in appearance from the sand that surrounded it.

After a moment, Vanth kicked the chest over, surrendering its contents to the shifting desert wind, and watched as it blew away.

TWENTY-THREE

THE MANDALORIAN brought the N-1 out of hyperspace and swooped down over the lush green mountains of the forested world of Ossus. Entering the planet's atmosphere, he heard the buzz from the navigation system and followed the beacon into position, settling the fighter into a flat space next to a river. He switched off the engines.

On the ground, the astromech droid R2-D2 waited for him, chirping in binary language, retracting the antenna he'd used to guide Mando down.

Mando climbed out of the cockpit. "Hello, friend," he said. "I'm looking for Skywalker."

R2-D2 beeped in response.

"I came to see the kid, Grogu."

The droid trilled and whistled, then spun to lead him away. Mando followed, and they made their way through the flat terrain into a forest of reedy trees and fallen leaves. The woods were tranquil and quiet, silent except for the soft rustle of wind in the branches.

After a while, Mando saw a large ant droid crawling over the hill, its six legs moving up and down like pistons to carry it along. Through the clearing, he observed more ant droids, a dozen or more, all laboring industriously to build a stony structure in the distance.

"Is this where they are?" Mando asked.

Instead of answering, R2-D2 spoke briefly to one of the ant droids, then put himself into hibernation mode and fell silent.

"Hey, droid," Mando said as the ant droids continued to march past him, up and down the hillside. "Don't shut off. Wake up." He waved one hand in front of R2-D2's sensors and sighed. Meanwhile, several of the ant droids were approaching, holding rocks and tree stalks in their mandibles. "Hey, I'm looking for Skywalker," Mando told one of them. "He had a kid with him?" He looked more closely at what the droids were constructing, a row of stalks across the stacked rocks. "Is that a bench? How long will I be waiting?"

Another droid placed a thatch of soft leaves on top of the bench.

“Is anyone here?” Mando asked, raising his voice as he looked back at the stone structure on the hillside. “Anyone alive?”

Glancing at the hibernating astromech unit, Mando sat down on his bench.

In an open meadow on another part of the planet, Luke Skywalker sat facing Grogu, both with their eyes closed, meditating in the shade of a nearby tree. The silence was disturbed by a rustling in the grass, and Grogu opened his eyes, distracted by the sound of an approaching frog. The child turned to watch the frog, then after a moment he levitated it into the air, bringing it nearer.

The frog croaked, twirling and kicking its legs as Grogu guided it toward his open mouth. Luke opened his eyes and saw what was happening.

“Grogu,” the Jedi Master said with a touch of reproach.

The child looked at him, dutifully chastened. The frog dropped to the ground and hopped into a pond with a splash. Luke regarded the child for a moment, then closed his eyes and raised one hand toward the pond. Moments later, Grogu’s eyes widened as a flotilla of frogs rose from the water, wiggling and kicking in the air. Luke made a small gesture, and the frogs fell into the water again.

Luke stood. "All right," he said, "let's go for a walk."

They started down the path through the trees, Luke helping Grogu along while the child took a series of little levitating hops to keep pace with the Jedi Master's stride.

"I want to tell you about someone you remind me of a great deal," Luke told him. "His name was Yoda. He was small like you, but his heart was huge, and the Force was strong in him. He once said to me, 'Size matters not.'" Luke looked down at Grogu. "That's how he talked. He would speak in riddles. Have you heard anyone talk like that back home?"

Grogu peered up at him in silence.

"Do you remember back home?" Luke asked, bending down to the child's level. "Would you like to remember?" He placed one hand on Grogu's wrinkled head. "Let me help you remember."

Closing his eyes, the child ventured into his own past. In the depths of his memory, he saw three Jedi Knights defending their temple from a battalion of clone troopers. The air was thick with smoke and blaster fire. As the 501st Clone Battalion advanced, the

Jedi fell, one by one, before the troopers' blasters in an attempt to protect Grogu.

He opened his eyes again and saw Luke looking at him.

"Welcome back," the Jedi Master said kindly. They were sitting in front of a pond with the mountains around them in the distance. "The galaxy is a dangerous place, Grogu. I will teach you to protect yourself."

Lying on his leafy bench, Mando heard a twig snap and grabbed his blaster, pointing it in the direction of the noise.

The Togruta woman stood watching him. Her skin was orange, with distinctive white markings, and the blue stripes of her head-tails draped over her shoulders. Mando recognized her immediately as Ahsoka Tano. She stood with her arms crossed.

He sat up. "You," he said. "I didn't expect to see you here."

"I'm an old friend of the family," Ahsoka said.

"I thought you weren't going to help train Grogu," Mando said.

"I'm not," she said. "Master Luke is."

"Then what are you doing here?"

"That's my question for you," she said, walking over to him.

"I'm here to see the kid."

Ahsoka placed an affectionate hand on the dome of R2-D2, who had just woken up. "That's why Artoo brought you to me instead," she said, and the droid let out an appreciative bleep.

"What is this place?" Mando asked, indicating the stone building on the knoll, where the ant droids were still crawling and working away.

"It's nothing now," Ahsoka said, "but someday it will be a great school. Grogu will be its first student."

"I'd like to know how he's doing," Mando said.

Ahsoka looked at him cautiously. "He's doing fine."

"I want to see him."

She sighed. "I know you do," she said. "Let's take a walk." As they made their way through the forest, Ahsoka glanced over at Mando. "I warned you when we met that your attachment to Grogu would be difficult to let go of."

"He was a Mandalorian foundling in my care," Mando said. "I just want to make sure he's safe."

"There is no place in the galaxy more safe than here with Luke."

"I don't understand why you're all right with

Skywalker's decision to train the kid when you wouldn't," Mando said.

She stopped walking and turned to look at him, exhaling sharply. "Because it was his choice. I don't control the wants of others."

"Then it's my choice to go and see him," Mando said.

"Of course," she said. "If that is what you wish."

Following her gaze through the trees, Mando found himself looking at two figures in the distance, sitting beneath a tree. The larger one was Skywalker, and the smaller was Grogu.

"All right," Mando said, and started walking toward them.

"Are you doing this for Grogu?" Ahsoka asked behind him. "Or are you doing this for yourself?"

Mando stopped. "I just want to give him this," he said, taking out the small cloth bundle he'd brought with him.

"Why? So that he will remember you?"

"No," Mando said. "As a Mandalorian foundling, he should have this. It's his right."

"Foundling," Ahsoka repeated thoughtfully. "Perhaps he is a Padawan now."

Mando was quiet for a moment, considering her words. "Well, either way, this armor will protect him."

"If you are set on it," Ahsoka said, "then allow me to deliver it."

"I came all this way," Mando said, staring up at the tiny figure of the child seated on the hillside in the distance. "And he's right there."

Ahsoka stepped toward him and placed her hand on his shoulder. "Grogu misses you a great deal," she said gently. "If he sees you, it will only make things more difficult for him."

Slowly, the Mandalorian reached out and gave her the cloth bundle. "Make sure he's protected." Then, after taking one final look at the child on the hillside, he turned to go.

TWENTY-FOUR

FROM HIS PERCH on Luke's back, Grogu saw the starfighter speeding away from the planet. He raised one hand as it flew off.

"All right," Luke said, putting the child down. "It's time to continue your training. Let's see you jump."

Grogu bent down and executed a small hop, barely getting his feet off the ground.

"Really?" Luke said, hands on hips. "That's all you got?" He gestured outward. "Bend down, jump, and as you do, feel the Force flow through you."

Grogu bent down and managed another small hop.

"You're trying too hard," Luke said. "Don't try. Do." He picked up the backpack that he'd been carrying the child in. "Come on, I want to show you something."

Moments later, the child was strapped to his back as Luke ran through the forest, leaping and somersaulting over rocks and jumping off the back of a partially submerged large-mouthed mud yak. He began climbing a tree, scaling it to the top, where Grogu peered over Luke's shoulder at the mountaintops in the distance.

"Look," Luke said. "The wide world exists in balance. Feel the Force all around you." He closed his eyes, breathing. "Through the Force, you will find balance, as well."

The training continued with Grogu standing on a branch protruding out over the river, balancing on one foot, while Luke spoke encouragingly to him. Later, in the woods, Luke demonstrated lightsaber dueling moves, the green blade sweeping and swinging, reflecting in the child's eyes.

"This is a training remote," he said, placing a ball in front of the child. Grogu reached over and rolled it across the ground.

"No, that isn't how it works," Luke said, raising one hand. "*This* is how it works."

With a hiss, the remote came to life and flew into the air. The child gazed up at it curiously as the remote turned, rotated, and fired a laser beam at Grogu, startling him and making him jump aside and fall over.

"Get back up," Luke said. "Always get back up."

This time, when the remote fired at him, Grogu leapt aside first, doing a quick midair spin before landing safely.

"Good," Luke said, pleased. They were approaching the river, and Grogu hopped from rock to rock with the remote hovering above him. After dodging its lasers through a series of quick jumps and spins, the child raised one hand toward the remote and halted it midflight, holding it in position until it finally shorted out and fell into the water, smoking.

On the banks of the river, Ahsoka had joined Luke to observe the training exercise. "You taught him well," she said.

"It's more like he's remembering than I'm actually teaching him anything," Luke said.

"Sometimes the student guides the master."

They stood side by side at the water's edge, observing the child in silence, and then Luke spoke again. "The Mandalorian was here," he said.

"As I told you," Ahsoka said, "the two share a strong bond. And"—she held out her hand—"he brought him a gift."

Luke took the bundle of fabric from her and returned his attention to Grogu, still seated on a rock in the middle of the river. "Sometimes I wonder if his heart is in it."

"So much like your father," Ahsoka observed.

"What should I do about him?"

"Trust your instincts," she said, and turned to leave.

"Will I see you again?"

"Perhaps," she said. "May the Force be with you."

Luke pondered the bundle she'd put in his hand as she departed.

TWENTY-FIVE

RETURNING TO TATOOINE, the Mandalorian flew down over Boba Fett's palace and brought the N-1 in for a landing inside the hangar. As he got out, a Gamorrean guard walked over to meet him with a suspicious grunt, his ax at the ready.

"I'm here at the request of Fennec Shand," Mando said.

Nodding, the guard turned to lead him into the throne room. There, using a hologram map as illustration, Fennec Shand was conducting a briefing with the group Fett had assembled: the Mods, Krrsantan, and Mok Shaiz's majordomo.

"The Pyke Syndicate has been gathering soldiers in the last few weeks," Fennec said. "Mayor Mok Shaiz is on their payroll and has flown offworld, which leads us to believe the storm is about to break."

“It was a scheduled vacation, actually,” the majordomo piped up.

Silencing him with a glare, Fennec continued. “Here’s a map of where they are gathering”—she gestured at the hologram—“based on whispers. The three crime families of Mos Espa seem willing to lay low and let the Pykes move on our territory.” Turning, she directed the group’s attention toward the stairwell, where Mando stood listening. “This is the Mandalorian, Din Djarin. Thanks to him and Krrsantan, we now have enough experienced muscle to act as enforcers. The Mods have done a thorough job of surveying the streets, but we lack the numbers to cover our territory if an all-out war comes.” She shook her head. “We need foot soldiers.”

“I might be able to help with that,” Mando said.

Later, as he circled over Mos Pelgo, Mando looked down at the Jawas’ sandcrawler with the bleached skull of the krayt dragon tied on top of it. Seeing the skull brought back memories of his last visit there, and the battle he’d fought alongside the local citizenry and the Sand People to defeat the dragon. He landed the

N-1 outside the settlement and was climbing out when he saw a young bearded deputy coming out of the marshal's office, approaching him suspiciously.

"You wanna park your starship," the deputy said, "you gotta do it out there in the flats."

"I'm looking for Marshal Vanth," Mando said.

The man stopped and squinted at him. "I don't think you heard what I said."

"I heard you."

"I'll take it from here, Deputy," Cobb Vanth said, stepping into view behind the younger man. He smiled, eyebrows raised, as the deputy walked back inside. "He's new," he explained to Mando. "Still a bit jumpy." Then he pointed at the N-1 with genuine interest. "Is that a Naboo starfighter?"

"That's what it started off as," Mando said as the two men stood side by side, admiring the modified ship. "I haven't seen you since you gave up your armor. How have you been?"

"More careful," Vanth said. "Where's the little guy?"

"Back with his own folk," Mando said.

"That's too bad. I guess we both lost something we were fond of."

Mando waited, letting the silence play out. "Can I buy you a drink?"

They made their way back inside the same cantina where the two of them had first met, and the Weequay bartender filled two glasses while Mando explained the situation. When he'd finished, Vanth shook his head.

"I still don't see what all that's got to do with me," he said.

"I need you to lead a garrison," Mando said. "Your people are good fighters, and there's plenty of credits in it for them, too."

The marshal sat down across from him. "The peace is intact, Mando. We took out that dragon. My people don't want to fight anymore."

"Your town might be good for now," Mando pointed out, "but it's all part of the same planet. We need good people to step up, or the spice is bound to come through these parts."

"As long as I'm here, that's not a problem." Vanth sipped his drink and put the glass down on the table. "So why should they risk their lives for this Boba Fett?"

"Mos Pelgo might be good right now—"

"Freetown," the bartender interrupted.

Mando glanced at Vanth. "What?""

"It's called Freetown now," the marshal told him.

"We changed the name," the bartender said. "Suits us better."

“Well,” Mando said, “I fought side by side with the citizens of Freetown, and they’re brave people, and the Pyke Syndicate has us outnumbered, and we need your help.”

“The town wants no part of it,” the bartender insisted. “That’s a city folk fight.”

Mando returned his attention to the man sitting across the table from him. “Is that what you say, too, Marshal?”

“We’re square, you and me,” Vanth said.

“Yes, we are,” Mando said. “But I didn’t think you were one to back down from bullies.”

“See, that’s what I like about you, Mando.” Cobb Vanth took another sip of his drink. “That big smile of yours lets you get away with anything.”

“There’s no easy way to ask for a favor,” Mando said.

Vanth chuckled and let out a breath. “I’ll tell you what. Things are tough around here, but I’ll see what I can do.”

Mando nodded and rose from the table.

As Vanth and the bartender stood watching Mando’s ship ascend skyward, the marshal turned to the bartender. “Get the word out,” Vanth said. “Get all the men and women of fighting age to come into town. I want to have a meeting."

"It's not our problem, Marshal," the bartender protested.

"No," Vanth admitted, "but it might be, after they hear what I'm gonna say."

Reluctantly, the bartender went back inside to notify the others. Vanth stood for a moment listening to the wind chime tinkling overhead, and then he turned to squint out past the outskirts of town, into the open desert.

A lone figure in a wide-brimmed hat was making his way into town. He wore a long black coat that blew out behind him, his silhouette rippling in the heat that rose from the dunes.

"Hey, Jo," Vanth said to the woman working on a speeder bike in front of the office.

"Afternoon, Marshal."

"Do me a favor and tell these people to head inside for a spell."

She frowned, concerned. "Something wrong, Marshal?"

"I hope not," Vanth said. "Just rather err on the side of safety."

As Jo ushered the townspeople inside, Vanth

stepped out into the middle of the street to watch the stranger approach. From the doorway of the marshal's office, the deputy who had first met Mando stepped into view.

"What's going on, boss?"

"Let me handle this, Deputy," Vanth said.

The man from the desert had stopped walking. His head was tipped down so the brim of his hat shielded his eyes, but Vanth could hear his low, drawling voice clearly enough.

"Cobb Vanth," he said.

"And who might you be?" Vanth could see the lower part of the speaker's face now, the smooth blue-green skin and lipless mouth. Black breathing tubes protruded from either side of his elongated jaw.

"Whatever Fett is paying you," the stranger snarled, baring his teeth, "we'll match. And all you've got to do is stay put and let things play out."

"Hey, the marshal ain't for sale," the deputy called out as he stepped from the doorway again. Vanth glared at him and sighed, then returned his attention to the gunslinger in the street.

"I'm sorry, I didn't catch your name."

The stranger raised his head to reveal large red

eyes, the eyes of the Duros bounty hunter and mercenary known across the galaxy as Cad Bane.

"I'd be careful where I was sticking my nose if I were you," he said.

"Is that friendly advice, or a threat?" Vanth asked him.

"Boba Fett is a cold-blooded killer who worked with the Empire," Bane said.

"You tell your spice runners Tatooine is closed for business," the marshal said. "This planet's seen enough violence."

"You should've never given up your armor." Bane drew back the flap of his coat, revealing the pistol at his hip.

Vanth's hand crept back slowly to touch his blaster. On the porch, the deputy stood anxiously glancing back and forth between them as the standoff continued. From the corner of his eye, Vanth could see the younger man's hand growing increasingly restless, hovering over his holster, itching to grab his gun. As he reached for it, Vanth glanced over to stop him, distracted only for an instant—but an instant was long enough.

TCHHOW!

Cad Bane shot the marshal, blowing him backward

off his feet. Turning, Bane opened fire on the deputy, blasting him into the wall, leaving the younger man's body sagging in a corner.

Lowering his blaster, Bane looked at the faces peering out from either side of the street. "Tatooine belongs to the Syndicate," he said in a voice loud enough to be heard by all those listening. "As long as the spice keeps running, everyone will be left alone."

Holstering his gun, he turned and walked away.

TWENTY-SIX

UP-TEMPO MUSIC PLAYED, glassware clinked, and the banter of relaxed conversation filled the room. It was a typical night at Garsa's Sanctuary, and the club was humming with drinkers and gamblers as the usual patrons gathered to pass the time.

The two Pyke enforcers walked in and made their way to a table in the back. One of them carried a cylindrical container that he placed on the floor beside him. A protocol droid took their drink orders, but when the Twi'lek staff members approached to inquire whether they'd like their helmets cleaned, the Pykes simply shook their heads.

On the small stage, the band played on. Gazing out across her domain, Garsa Fwip permitted herself a smile.

Across the room, she saw the two newly arrived Pykes stand up, even though they hadn't been served yet. In fact, they practically knocked over the protocol droid bringing their drinks to the table. Garsa frowned, watching them leave. Something was troubling about all this, but she couldn't quite put her finger on it.

"Oh, wait!" the protocol droid exclaimed, lifting the cylindrical container from the floor beneath the table. "You forgot your camtono—"

An instant later, an explosion ripped through the room, blasting the club to pieces in a deafening eruption of orange flame. Outside the Sanctuary, passersby on the street were flung aside like broken toys as the fireball expanded outward into the night. Debris scattered, and the fiery remains of the club blazed and smoked in the darkness.

Far from this act of violence, on the forest planet where Luke Skywalker was training Grogu, a different kind of sanctuary had taken shape. The small stone building the ant droids were constructing as a school for Jedi had finally been completed.

Inside the school's shaded, dome-shaped structure, Luke and Grogu sat facing each other on a floor mat. Luke brought out the package Ahsoka had given him and opened it, taking out a small chain mail jacket fashioned from the beskar spear.

"The Mandalorian wanted you to have this," Luke said, holding it up so the child could see it and then placing it on the mat. "But before you take it, I will give you a choice." He opened a small wooden box. "This is a lightsaber." Switching it on, he let the green glow of its blade burst forth in the space between them. "It belonged to my teacher, Master Yoda. And now"—he deactivated the blade—"I'm offering it to you."

The child stood up, peering at the two objects in front of him, the chain mail and the lightsaber, side by side.

"But you may choose only one," Luke continued. "If you choose the armor, you'll return to your friend, the Mandalorian. However, you will be giving in to attachment to those you love and forsaking the way of the Jedi. But if you choose the lightsaber, you will be the first student in my academy, and I will train you to be a great Jedi. It will take you many years to master the ways of the Force, and you may never see the Mandalorian again." Luke paused to allow the importance of this message to penetrate. "Because, Grogu, a short time for you is a lifetime for someone else."

Grogu cooed, lowering his ears as the weight of the decision came to rest on his tiny shoulders. He looked back and forth between the chain mail and the lightsaber as Luke spoke the words that would ultimately determine the child's destiny.

"Which do you choose?"

IN THE NAME OF HONOR

TWENTY-SEVEN

THE FOLLOWING MORNING Boba Fett and Fennec Shand examined the bombed-out wreckage of the Sanctuary, along with Drash and Skad from the Mods. The four of them walked through the charred ruins of the club, studying the damage the explosion had left behind—burned walls, blackened furniture, and a lingering, deadly silence.

"We are at war," Fett said.

"It was inevitable," Fennec agreed.

"Even if we win," Fett said as he made his way through the charred debris of tables and chairs, "there might not be anything left of this city."

There was a scrape of footsteps behind them, and Fennec turned to see the Mandalorian standing in the doorway.

"That was fast," she said. "Were you able to hire any foot soldiers?"

"I think so," Mando said as he advanced to join the others. "Cobb Vanth is raising a garrison for us."

"What price did you negotiate?"

"Free," Mando said.

Fett frowned at him. *"Free?"*

"He's been holding off the spice trade single-handedly," Mando told them. "I told him we could shut it down."

"That's not free," Fennec objected. "That's most of Jabba the Hutt's business."

"That's what the town wants," Mando said.

Fett nodded. "I agree to their terms."

"There's a lot of credits to be made from that orange powder," Fennec told them.

"In the long run, it's better for us, as well," Fett said. "Mos Espa can become a prosperous city under our protection. Spice is killing our people." He looked at the Mandalorian. "Let Marshal Vanth and the people of Mos Pelgo know that—"

"Freetown is its name now," Mando said.

Fett nodded. "Let the people of Freetown know that they have my word."

"You can tell Cobb Vanth himself when he arrives here with the reinforcements," Mando said.

"You are confident he will come?"

"I am," Mando said.

"Well, if he does not," Fett said, "we are doomed. Our skill is no match for the Syndicate numbers. We must buy time until they arrive. We'll lock down at the palace."

"It's a bad idea," Skad interjected.

Fett turned to look at him. "And where do you propose to wait for reinforcements?"

"Here," Skad said.

"Here, in these ruins?" Fett scoffed. "Nonsense. The palace offers greater protection."

"If you want to abandon Mos Espa and hide in your fortress," Drash spoke up boldly, "go ahead. We're staying." The look in her eye was one of pure determination. "The people who live here need our protection."

After considering her words, Boba Fett exchanged glances with Fennec and the Mandalorian and then nodded.

"We'll stay," he said.

TWENTY-EIGHT

CAD BANE WALKED the streets of Mos Eisley in the dark, his red eyes gleaming beneath the brim of his hat. Somewhere in the shadows, a pair of Jawas saw him coming and cowered in fear as Bane strode into the Desert Survey Office.

"I have to respond," Mayor Mok Shaiz was saying as Bane entered. "I have to respond in some way. At the very least, I should—"

His voice broke off as he saw Bane entering the room. The Pyke crime boss Shaiz had been speaking to turned to look at the bounty hunter.

"You returned so quickly," the Pyke said. "Was your venture successful?"

"You won't have to worry about Freetown," Bane said.

"Did you convince the marshal to remain neutral?" the mayor asked.

Bane's teeth shone in a predatory smile. "Yes."

"Good," Shaiz said nervously. "I want this over as soon as possible. Does Fett have any other resources to call upon? He used to live among a Tusken Raider tribe in the desert."

"They no longer exist," the Pyke boss told him.

"Are you sure?"

"Yes. We destroyed them ourselves."

"Does Fett know that?" Bane asked.

"He has no idea," the Pyke assured him. "He thinks they were killed by Nikto speed bikers. We left evidence behind to encourage such a conclusion. He took his revenge on them. In his mind, the matter is resolved."

"I didn't realize the Pyke Syndicate was so ruthless," Bane said.

"Pragmatic," the Pyke boss amended. "They were charging us for protection. We have to protect our margins."

"Indeed you do," Bane agreed.

"So when will this all be over?" the mayor asked.

"That all depends on how much your two stomachs can bear," Bane said, referring to the Ithorian's dual digestive anatomy.

"No more explosions," Shaiz said. "I didn't sign off

on bombing Garsa's Sanctuary. I agreed to surgical strikes, not open warfare."

"With apologies," the Pyke boss said, "it seems that line has been crossed."

"Well, I am still the mayor of Mos Espa," Shaiz said, "and I will not see it destroyed."

"The Fett gotra is taking refuge in the ruins of the Sanctuary," the Pyke said. "It will take extreme measures to remove them."

Bane regarded them for a moment. "I think I have an idea how to draw Boba Fett out," he said.

TWENTY-NINE

INSIDE HANGAR THREE-FIVE, Peli Motto's hibernating crew of pit droids popped up on high alert, sounding the alarm. Their scanners had picked up the proximity beacon of an incoming spacecraft, and when Peli checked the monitor screen, she couldn't believe her eyes.

"It's an X-wing!" she said inside the control room, staring at the outline on the screen. "What's an X-wing doing here?"

On the hangar floor, one of the pit droids raised a set of light sticks and began to guide the fighter downward.

"Stay in here," Peli said to R5-D4, climbing out of the control booth. "Lock it up, will you?" She gestured frantically at a crate of contraband equipment. "Hide that! Get rid of that! Get moving. You heard me—*go!*"

As the X-wing settled onto the landing pad and the

canopy popped open, Peli ran toward it, waving her hands in the air.

"Hello, officer!" she called out in what she hoped was her friendliest and most law-abiding voice. "I filed for my New Republic certification seal just as you were landing. Quite a coincidence, if you ask me."

She waited for a response, but the face peering down from the cockpit wasn't a New Republic pilot's. It was the tiny wrinkled head of Mando's young companion, his ears twitching slightly as he gazed down at her and babbled out a greeting.

"Well, look who it is!" Peli broke out in a chuckle and started climbing up the ladder. "Aw, did they teach you how to fly an X-wing already?"

Behind her on the ground, R5-D4 let out a disapproving electronic grumble, and Peli glared back at him. "I know an astromech flew the ship," she said.

In the X-wing's astromech socket, R2-D2 chirped out a question.

"The Mandalorian?" Peli said. "He's not here." When the droid asked another question, she shook her head. "I don't know—he's on a job in Mos Espa. But just slow down. Give me a second. You just got here. Let me say hello to my old pal."

The child gurgled at her happily.

"Well, hello, bright eyes! Come here!" As she lifted him up, R2-D2 made another series of whistles and beeps.

"Grogu?" Peli said. "Whoa! That's a *terrible* name. Sorry about that, pal. No way am I calling you that." She pulled down the collar of the child's tunic to look at the gleaming chain mail underneath. "What do you have under here, something shiny? Well, look at you, all fancy. You must be starving." Turning, she shouted at the droids, "Bring him some dung worms!"

R2-D2 interjected with a burst of binary.

"Oh, keep your dome on!" Peli said. "I don't care how big of a rush you're in. Baby's gotta eat." She settled in with the child and the droids as Grogu helped himself to a bucket of dung worms, cooing with satisfaction as they slithered into his mouth.

THIRTY

INSIDE THE RUINS of the Sanctuary, Boba Fett and the others listened as Fennec Shand briefed them on her plans.

"As we wait for the reinforcements to arrive with Cobb Vanth from Freetown," she said, "our forces are quietly patrolling the streets of the old city. The Pyke Syndicate has not yet arrived in numbers, but the minute they do, we will see them before they see us." She turned to Boba Fett. "The truce you negotiated with the other families of Mos Espa will ensure that they remain neutral and allow us to gain the upper hand by surprising the arriving soldiers."

She went on to tell them how the Gamorrean guards were posted in the Klatooinian territory, where they would send an early warning if any of the Pyke forces arrived. In Trandoshan territory, Krrsantan was keeping tabs on the streets of the municipality in front of City Hall. Drash and Skad were with the other Mods, keeping an eye on the Worker's District and the Aqualish Quarter.

"As you can see," Fennec concluded, "all our flanks are covered. Nobody is sneaking up on us. When the people of Freetown arrive, we will have the forces required to pivot our strength to whatever region the Pykes choose to attack from."

"For now?" Fett asked.

"We wait," Fennec said.

"Lord Fett," 8D8 spoke up. "There is someone here to see you."

Fett grimaced. "I thought you said nobody could sneak up on us," he said. He put his helmet on and walked up the steps and out the front door of the Sanctuary, into the daylight, then stopped.

Standing at the far end of the street was Cad Bane.

"I thought I smelled something," Fett said. "If you're looking for a job, you're late."

"I've already got a job," Bane said. "I'm here to negotiate on behalf of the Pyke Syndicate."

"I don't negotiate with gutless murderers," Fett said.

"If that's not the Quacta calling the Stifling slimy," Bane sneered.

"Clear out," Fett said. "And tell your bosses we know they're outnumbered."

"I wouldn't be counting on the people of Freetown to be coming anytime soon," Bane told him. "I paid Marshal Vanth a visit. You should've never left him without his armor."

Fett stood listening to the killer's words, understanding their meaning all too well. From either side of the entrance behind Fett, Fennec and the Mandalorian crept into view, blasters at the ready.

"Before you get any ideas," Bane said, "I've got back shooters, too."

Looking up, Fett saw Pyke snipers rising into view from the balconies above the street where Bane stood, two on either side.

"Let the spice move through Mos Espa," Bane said, "and all this can be avoided."

Fett waited for a moment before responding. "No."

"What do you propose then?"

"I will only negotiate with the head of the Pyke Syndicate."

"You mean the one that massacred your Tusken family," Bane asked, "and blamed it on a speed bike gang?"

Fett's mind flashed to the scorched ruins of the Tusken camp and the insignia painted so boldly on the flap of the tent.

Bane grinned. "You know it's true."

Boba Fett raised his blaster, and Fennec stepped closer. "Boba . . ." she cautioned.

"Let's do this," Bane said as he drew back his long coat to reveal the blasters strapped to either hip, his fingers wiggling over the handles. "Right here, right now."

"Not now," Fennec advised where she stood behind Fett. "You pick when."

"He killed Vanth," Fett told her. "The reinforcements aren't coming."

"We fight on our terms, not theirs."

"I can take him," Fett said.

Fennec's voice remained steady. "You're emotional."

"I can take him."

"We need to adjust," she said, enunciating every word. "You'll have your moment."

Slowly Fett raised one hand to place it on top of his blaster. "Tell your client negotiations are terminated."

"You're going soft in your old age," Bane said.

"We all do," Fett said.

As Cad Bane turned and walked away, Boba Fett made his way back to the entrance of the Sanctuary. The mayor's majordomo was already headed out to meet him.

"That was an impressive display of restraint," the Twi'lek gushed. "Exemplary stratagem. If I may be so bold as to offer additional counsel . . ."

"I wonder how much he would pay for the Twi'lek," Fett muttered.

"Understood. Many pardons. I should never have interjected."

"Come in, boss." A voice crackled from Fett's comm. It was Drash, one of the Mods, and she sounded deeply concerned. "Something feels strange over here."

"Have the Pykes arrived?" Fett asked.

"Not yet," Drash said. "But something feels off. It's—"

The rest of the message was lost in a storm of blaster fire and shouts.

"The locals are attacking!" Drash spoke sharply into the communicator. She and the other Mods were pinned down at the end of an alleyway while a group of Aqualish in the Worker's District pulled hidden weapons from barrels and opened fire on them.

Outside the Sanctuary, the Mandalorian stared at Boba Fett. "I thought we had a treaty!"

"So did I," Fett said.

"They laid a trap!" Drash shouted as a blaster bolt flew past her and struck one of the Mods in the chest, knocking him down.

Boba Fett raised the comm to his helmet. "Santo," he said. "Santo, come in!"

From his position in front of City Hall, Krrsantan growled as the scene before him erupted into chaos. A gang of Trandoshans were drawing swords and melee weapons and attacking the crowds around them, sending the citizens of the area running for cover. Before Krrsantan could respond to the threat, the Trandoshans jumped on top of the Wookiee, overwhelming him and forcing him to the ground.

At the same time, the two Gamorrean guards stationed in front of a hovertrain saw a group of Klatooinians waiting to ambush them. The Klatooinians charged forward with spears, lunging and jabbing, forcing the Gamorreans backward and sending them plummeting over the edge of a cliff with horrified squeals.

"It's a coordinated attack," Fett said inside the Sanctuary. "We'll have to gather our people."

"There's no way to overcome their advantage,"

Fennec said. "We need to take out command and control."

Fett turned to the mayor's majordomo. "Does the Pyke Syndicate still operate out of Mos Eisley?" he demanded.

"Oh, it's difficult to say for certain," the majordomo said, and when Fennec cocked her rifle, his voice rose an octave in panic. "Mos Eisley? Yes, yes, now that I think of it, indeed they do! More specifically, the Desert Survey Office."

"Can you do that?" Fett asked Fennec. "Can you get there in time?"

"Worth a shot," she said, and ran to her speeder bike.

In the Worker's District, the situation in the alleyway was falling apart further by the second. Drash, Skad, and the Mods were cornered by Aqualish fighters who'd left them with no place to run, and a shooter in an overhead window was pouring blaster fire down from above.

"How many are there?" Drash asked.

"I can't tell," Skad said. "At least a dozen."

CHHZZAOOWW! Another series of shots hammered the wall behind them, slamming into one of the Mods and cutting him down.

"We can't retreat!" Drash shouted into the comm. "We're pinned down!"

"Stay put," Fennec responded through the transmitter.

"What?"

"Don't move!"

"But they'll swamp our position!" Drash said frantically as the firefight blazed around her.

"Keep your heads down!" Fennec ordered.

KCHOWW-CHOWW! Blaster fire tore through the air, hitting the Aqualish shooters and eliminating three of them in as many seconds. Startled and overwhelmed, the remaining assailants turned and fled, and the sniper in the window hardly had time to react before another shot knocked him from his perch and sent him tumbling down onto some buckets of water.

From where they were standing, Drash, Skad, and the remaining Mods looked up to see Fennec Shand stepping into view with her rifle. Fennec leapt through the air, executed a neat midair spin, and landed on her feet next to her speeder bike.

"Get to the Sanctuary," she told them.

"Hey," Drash said, approaching her. "Thank you."

"Manners." Fennec lowered the visor on her helmet. "I like it. You're welcome."

She hit the bike's throttle and sped off.

Outside the Sanctuary, the Pyke Syndicate forces began to move into position, coming down the street and taking up posts on top of the buildings nearby.

"They're here," Mando said.

"It was just a matter of time," Fett said. "Is Cad Bane with them?"

Mando gazed through the crack in the door. "Don't see him. Any news on the others?"

"It would be a miracle if any survived," Fett said grimly. "All three gotras of Mos Espa turned on us."

"It was the smart move," Mando said.

"It was." Fett nodded. "I suppose you'll be heading out."

"I'm not."

"You should."

"It's against the Creed," Mando told him. "I gave you my word. I'm with you until we both fall."

"You really buy into that bantha fodder?" Fett asked.

"I do," Mando said, and Boba Fett nodded.

"Good."

"The way I see it," Mando continued, "we have two choices. We wait until they get into position and launch a siege on their terms."

"Or?"

"We rush out there," the Mandalorian said, "catch them unaware. Then we can escape to your ship at the palace."

"I can't abandon Mos Espa," Fett said. "These people are counting on me."

"Okay, then," Mando said. "We'll both die in the name of honor."

"You sure you wanna stay?" Fett asked.

Mando raised his blaster. "This is the Way," he said, and turned to point his pistol out the doorway, finger on the trigger, preparing to open fire.

"If I may offer an alternative?" the majordomo spoke up, and everyone turned to look at him as he stepped forward, hands in the air. "Shall I continue? I'll continue." He drew in a deep breath. "You may not know this about me—in fact, how could you, except perhaps what vestiges remain of my accent?—but I was educated on Coruscant. Not that that makes me better in any way, but—"

"Get to it," Fett barked.

"I attended finishing academy," the Twi'lek went on, "although my parents were not wealthy by any means, and I specialized in civic council negotiations. Now, if you would feel confident empowering me to negotiate on your behalf, I'm fairly certain we would be granted passage offworld with, at worst, some theatrical, symbolic groveling gestures . . . and an exchange of funds."

Fett glanced at the Mandalorian, then looked over at the majordomo. "Very well," he said. "Give me your tablet. I will write out my statement and what I am willing to pay."

"I shall go as your emissary," the Twi'lek said enthusiastically, handing over the tablet. "I have no compunction whatsoever genuflecting or even groveling if needs be, which would save you from any potential bruising of ego, so to speak."

Fett finished writing and returned the tablet to the majordomo with a grunt. "Now go before I change my mind."

"Yes. Excellent," the Twi'lek said, and strode out the door, already raising his voice to address the heavily armed Pykes gathered immediately outside the Sanctuary. "Salutations!" he exclaimed. "I am unarmed, but for this tablet, bearing the terms of surrender I wish to present to whomever spokesperson is empowered to deliberate an acceptable outcome in the eyes of the Oba Diah high council."

"Read it to me, tail-head," the Pyke standing in front of him snapped.

The majordomo chortled mirthfully. "Oh, because of the . . ." He pointed to the pair of head-tails that furled down from either side of his skull. "Oh, enchanting sobriquet, and one of which I never tire. Yes, someday I hope to see the fabled Obsidian Cliffs of Oba Diah with my own eyes, and perhaps—"

"Read it."

"Agreed," the Twi'lek said. "Let us dispense with pleasantries." He cleared his throat and looked down at the tablet, reading aloud. "'I, Boba Fett, speaking as daimyo of the Tatooine territories, formerly held by Jabba the Hutt, do present the following offer. . . .'"

His voice trailed off as his eyes moved across what Fett had written next. He glanced hopefully up at the Pyke in front of him.

"Perhaps," he said, "we should discuss what *you'd* be willing to—"

"Read it!" the Pyke demanded.

"'. . . the following offer,'" the Twi'lek continued, and cleared his throat. "'Nothing. You will leave this planet'"—his voice was quavering audibly—"'and your spice trade. If you refuse these terms'"—he cleared his throat again before forcing himself onward in a strangled voice—"'the arid sands of Tatooine will once again flourish with flowered fields fertilized with the bodies of your dead.'"

The Pyke turned and looked at the enforcer standing next to him. Then he raised his blaster toward the majordomo.

"His words," the Twi'lek managed weakly.

ZZTCHHEWW! Sudden blaster fire tore down from overhead, and the majordomo gaped up in amazement to see Boba Fett and the Mandalorian sailing high above him, propelled by their jet packs, firing down at the Pykes. As the Twi'lek ran for cover, the Pyke shooters squinted up at Fett and Mando, unable to take accurate aim in the harsh glare of the midday suns.

Landing on the ground, Fett and Mando stood back to back, picking off the enemy with pinpoint accuracy. More Pyke soldiers poured out from behind the buildings as the fighting grew heavier. Blaster shots pinged and ricocheted off Mando's beskar, knocking him off his feet. He raised his wrist and released the whistling birds, the storm of tiny, lethal darts taking out several Pykes at once, and a moment later followed it up with a rocket that blasted another assailant to pieces, along with the building behind him.

"They just keep coming!" Fett said. Within moments the assault had driven them both to their knees as heavier firepower overwhelmed their efforts. Blasters hammered their armor from all sides, pinning them down.

Then, out of nowhere, a blaster shot hit one of the Pykes, and Mando and Fett both sat up in surprise to see a large armored speeder roaring around the corner.

"The people of Freetown!" Mando said. Aboard the speeder, the citizens of Freetown were aiming and firing at the Pykes. Mando saw the Weequay bartender at the front of the speeder, hunched behind a turret gun pouring out a continuous flow of blaster fire while others shot from both sides, driving back the Pykes.

Pulling up alongside Mando and Fett, the speeder stopped. "Out, while we've got cover!" the bartender shouted, and the Freetown reinforcements jumped off and took cover behind it, still blasting away at the Pykes while Fett and Mando joined them. Within moments, they'd driven the last of the Syndicate backward, and the street fell silent.

"I'm sorry about the marshal," Mando said to the bartender.

"Gunned him down in cold blood," the bartender said, his voice tight with anger.

"You didn't have to come here."

"Yes, we did." The bartender sighted his rifle at a Pyke fighter on the far end of the street and squeezed off another shot. "This planet deserves better."

The whine of grav scoots approached, and Mando saw the Mods roaring toward the remaining Pykes, firing on them from the other side. One of the Syndicate gunmen scored a direct hit on Skad's scoot, flipping it over and sending him tumbling as he scrambled to join Drash and the others behind the makeshift barricade of the armored speeder.

Skad glanced suspiciously up at the Freetown people. "Where'd all these sand scurriers come from?"

"We're here to save the tails of some city rats," the Freetowner named Jo retorted.

"Save it for the Pykes," Fett told them.

A howling snarl erupted from around the corner as two Pyke shooters flailed helplessly through the air, and Fett saw Krrsantan charging into view. The gladiator Wookiee was in full berserker mode, smashing the Syndicate's hired muscle and tossing them in all directions. He grabbed one of the Pykes, tossed him up, and blasted him out of the air, then used another Pyke as a projectile, flinging him hard at the shooters immediately in front of him.

But he was badly injured, Fett saw—limping, dragging his right leg, and struggling to go forward. Blasters smashed into him from either side, and at last the Wookiee fell in the street.

"Cover me!" Fett shouted, running out to grab Krrsantan and help him to safety.

"Welcome back, Santo," he said. "I have to confess, I thought you were gone. I owe you a nice long soak in the bacta tank when this is done."

"They're falling back!" the bartender shouted, and the fighters cheered.

Mando tapped the sensor on his helmet and saw insectoid shapes approaching in the distance.

"I wouldn't celebrate yet," he said. "We've got problems." He watched as two massive Scorpenek droids made their way into the street, their armored mechanized legs clanging as they approached. "We've got *real* problems."

THIRTY-ONE

THE SCORPENEKS had already activated their deflector shields. No matter how much Fett, Mando, and the others fired on them, the blaster bolts bounced harmlessly off the lethal war droids. Meanwhile their onboard blaster cannons were tearing the street apart as they advanced toward the barricade in front of the Sanctuary.

Mando used his scope to target the red eye in the center of one Scorpenek's processing center and fired a rocket that sent up a ball of flame. But when the smoke cleared, the droids kept coming.

"Run!" Mando told the Freetowners. "We'll distract them!"

There was a deafening *THHOOOM!* as one of the droid's cannons scored a direct hit on the Freetown speeder, reducing it to a twisted pile of metal. Mando and Fett used their jet packs to go airborne, landing on the opposite side of the Scorpeneks to renew their attack. Fett assaulted them with rapid fire from his blaster, and Mando took out the Darksaber, but the black blade could do nothing against the deflectors.

"I can't get through!" he said.

"These two will destroy the whole city!" Fett shouted.

Mando understood the situation all too well. "Our energy weapons can't get through, and our kinetic weapons have too much velocity."

"Move!" Fett told him, and a second later, the place where they'd been standing was obliterated by a droid's cannons. "Can you protect the others?"

"I can distract them for a spell," Mando said. "Why?"

"We need reinforcements," Fett told him.

"From where? You've run out of friends."

"Protect the others!" Boba Fett ordered, and blasted into the sky.

Grunting, Mando ran between the Scorpeneks, still firing, leading one of them away from the fleeing Freetowners. As he ducked around a corner, he saw a RIC droid heading toward him, carrying the last person he'd expected to see under the circumstances.

"Mando!" Peli Motto exclaimed. She was seated in the carriage with her pit droids dangling off the sides. "Ha! We found you! I got a surprise for you."

"Turn around!" Mando shouted.

She looked at him, baffled. "What?"

"Turn around!"

Peli stared up at the Scorpenek coming around the corner, its cannons blazing. "Turn around!" she screamed. The RIC droid spun its wheels and went into a tight turn, spraying sand and dust as it whipped the carriage behind it and swerved in the opposite direction. Mando took another shot at the Scorpenek, then turned and ran after the RIC droid, jumping on the back of it.

"Can this thing go any faster?" he asked.

"Go faster, you bucket of bolts!" Peli shouted, and tossed a wrench at the droid's head. With a whoop, the droid took off at double speed.

The second Scorpenek chased the Freetown reinforcements, along with the Mods and Krrsantan, down the street, blasting the city to ruins around it.

"Take cover!" the Weequay bartender shouted, pointing toward the partially demolished remains of a house. Desperate to escape, the group ran inside and crouched behind a wall.

"We have to stop retreating!" Drash told Jo, who was positioned across the entryway from her. "We need to dig in here!"

Outside in the street, the bartender fired his cycler rifle at the droid while Krrsantan shot his blaster rifle, but none of the artillery was making a dent in the Scorpenek's shields.

"Fall back!" the bartender yelled. "We're getting swamped."

"She says we should stay," Jo told him.

"Nonsense, we'll get vaporized." The Weequay leaned over the wall with his rifle and attempted another shot.

"I grew up a womp-hop from here," Drash said, "and if we fall back any further, we'll be cornered with no cover."

A jet of flame whooshed down the street in front of the makeshift garrison, and the bartender stared at Drash. "So we're gonna die here?"

"No," Drash said, firing her blaster pistol over the wall. "We fight." She looked up at the balcony above them. "Skad, hold the line with the Weequay. I'll head up there and snipe down."

"Let me see that thing," Jo said, and Drash showed her the blaster pistol she held. "With *that*?" Jo shook her head and turned to the Weequay. "Taanti, we need a cycler."

The bartender passed his cycler rifle to Jo, who gave it to Drash.

"Good luck," he said.

"Let's go," Jo said.

Drash gripped the cycler, bracing to run. "Cover us," she told Skad, and they took off.

As the citizens of Freetown prepared to make their stand against the Scorpenek, Peli Motto's RIC droid careened through the city streets with the Mandalorian still clinging on, leaning over the front.

"Hey, Mando," Peli said, pulling back a blanket on the seat next to her. "Look who's here!" Grogu turned to look up at him, ears blowing in the breeze.

"What?" Mando said with a gasp. "Hey, what are you doing here?"

With a coo of delight, Grogu jumped up into the Mandalorian's arms, and Mando hugged him to his chest.

"Okay, little guy. I'm happy to see you, too. I didn't know when I'd see you again."

The child gurgled at him, reaching for Mando's helmet.

"Yeah, I missed you, too, buddy, but we're in a bit of a bind right now." Mando lowered Grogu back into the RIC droid's carriage. "Be careful. You keep your head down. You stay hidden until the fight's over." He caught a glimpse of polished beskar beneath the child's tunic. "Hey, that's the shirt. You got the shirt—"

SSCHHOWW! An explosion rocked the carriage.

"Save your tender moment!" Peli yelled. "We've got a Scorpenek droid chasing us!"

Turning, Mando opened fire on the droid advancing toward them. "What is he doing here?" he asked Peli.

"The Force works in mysterious ways," she said.

A blast from the Scorpenek's cannons tore the head off the RIC droid, and the carriage flipped end over end, propelling Mando, Peli, and the child through the air. Hitting his jet pack, Mando shot forward and managed to catch Grogu and land on his back, protecting the child from impact while he rolled over to keep shooting.

But it was no use. The Scorpenek towered over

them, cannons blasting, and there was nowhere left to run. Mando glanced up in time to see Peli roll over, spit out a tooth, and grab a blaster. She was tough; he'd give her that. If this was the end, then there wasn't a better bunch to go out with.

Then he heard the roar.

THIRTY-TWO

EVERYONE LOOKED UP.

Across the street, a huge three-clawed hand reached up to curl around the edge of a building as the rancor hoisted itself into view.

As the creature loomed over the Scorpenek droid, Mando looked up and saw Boba Fett astride its back, holding on to the reins. The Scorpenek opened fire, and the rancor jumped from the top of the building and landed on the ground in front of the droid. With another roar, it began slamming its claws against the droid's shielding with tremendous, shattering force.

Mando bent down and placed Grogu inside a doorway. "Don't move," he said. "Let me handle this." Drawing the Darksaber, he charged toward the Scorpenek, swinging the black blade at the weakened area where the rancor had damaged the droid's shielding.

He penetrated the shield, hit his jet pack, and blasted up on top of the Scorpenek's head. Through the remains of the shield, he could see the rancor's enraged face as the creature continued to pound on the battle droid with all its strength.

Mando swung the Darksaber, slicing off one of the Scorpenek's gun turrets, but the droid threw him off, turned, and clambered toward Mando, rearing up to crush him.

As it did so, Grogu stepped out from his hiding place. Closing his eyes, the child lifted one hand, and the Scorpenek froze at the top of its strike. Then Grogu pulled an articulation pin from the droid's leg. The dislodged pin flew and hit Grogu, knocking him backward.

The droid's unbolted leg flailed and creaked unsteadily as it tried to go after Mando again, but it was moving too crookedly to attack. The rancor landed in the street and began hammering the droid with its fists.

Mando scooped up Grogu protectively, and they watched together as the rancor lifted the Scorpenek, clutching it by its remaining arms.

"Do it," Fett commanded the creature.

With a roar, the rancor ripped the thing in half, and the droid exploded, spraying loose parts and shrapnel everywhere.

Drash and Jo had managed to climb onto the rooftop while the rest of the Mods and Freetowners made their stand against the second Scorpenek and the Syndicate shooters in the street below.

"Can you pick off some of the fighters?" Drash asked.

"I'm used to desert hunting," Jo said with a half smile. "Can't miss at this range."

Drash nodded. "I'll distract the droid."

She opened up with the cycler rifle on the Scorpenek, and Jo stood up and drew a bead on the Pyke shooters—taking out five of them in a series of perfect shots. When the Scorpenek reeled around and took aim at them, Drash and Jo exchanged glances of mutual understanding, and they both began firing at the droid.

Suddenly, the building to their left burst open in a deafening cascade of brick and concrete, and Drash saw a giant creature plow into view. It knocked the Scorpenek across the street, where it collided with a building that collapsed on top of it with a crash.

There was a moment of quiet, and the ruined building blew apart as the Scorpenek emerged, crawling forward to engage the rancor again. The rancor smashed it against a building, but the droid recovered, driving its legs against the creature's hide. Lunging forward, the rancor gripped the droid's gun turrets, then plunged one of its talons into the droid's single red eye.

The Scorpenek collapsed, and a cheer rose up from the Freetown people as the rancor picked up what remained of the droid and flung it into a building, where it exploded. Seeing the outcome of the battle, the Pyke fighters turned and fled.

"Keep 'em on their heels!" Mando shouted. "They're on the run!"

The Weequay bartender and the others sprang out from behind the wall, still firing, and began to pursue the Pykes down the street. Meanwhile, Peli had grabbed a blaster and joined them, but her head snapped around when she saw the Twi'lek majordomo peeking up at her from where he'd been hiding.

"I am not a threat!" the majordomo said, hands raised.

"Nice head-tails," Peli said admiringly. "Come on, get behind me, pretty face. Peli's got you covered."

The Twi'lek jumped up to follow her. "Pleasure to make your acquaintance."

"We don't have time for that," Peli grunted.

Above them, the rancor bellowed and roared, snatching the remaining Pyke fighters in its claws. It crushed one of them against a wall and held another one up so Boba Fett, who was still astride the creature's back, could blast him. Fett watched as the rancor grabbed another Pyke and shoved him headfirst into its mouth.

Then Fett saw Cad Bane step into the street.

When the rancor snarled and lunged at him, Bane raised one arm and unleashed a jet of flame into the beast's face. The rancor reared back in pain, recoiling violently enough to throw Boba Fett from its back. As Fett tumbled to the ground, Bane shot more fire at the rancor.

With a furious roar, the rancor turned and retreated from the flames.

Boba Fett rose to his feet and saw Bane standing there waiting for him. "Clear out," Fett told him as the two of them faced off in the street. "And take your hoodlum gang with you."

"I've known you a long time, Boba," Bane said. "One thing that I can't figure out. What's your angle?"

"This is my city," Fett said. "These are my people. I will not abandon them."

Cad Bane's face twisted into a toothy grin. "Like the Tuskens."

"Don't toy with me," Fett said. "I'm not a little boy any longer, and you are an old man."

"I'm still faster than you."

"That may be," Fett said, "but I have armor."

"Let's find out," Bane said. He drew back his coat, hand hovering over his pistol. When Fett raised his rifle, Bane's blaster was already out of the holster and firing, hitting Fett and throwing him back into the street.

"Now's about the time you jet off to your bacta tank," Bane growled as he sauntered toward Fett.

"This is my city!" Fett said, lunging up to attack with his flamethrower. Bane rolled out of its path, sprang up, and shot Fett again.

"You gave it a shot," Bane said as he made his way unhurriedly toward Fett, who lay in the dusty street, groaning with pain. "You tried to go straight. But you've got your father's blood pumping through your veins." The Duros mercenary was towering over Fett, the outline of hat and breathing tubes cutting an eerie silhouette against the twin suns. "*You're a killer.*"

He kicked Fett, knocking his rifle away.

"This isn't the first time I beat you out on a job," Bane said with a sneer. Placing his boot on Fett's gun hand, he knelt over him and tore off Fett's helmet, exposing his face. "There's no shame in it."

Fett stared up at him.

"Consider this my final lesson," Bane said. "Look out for yourself." He pointed his pistol at Fett's face. "Anything else is weakness."

Fett closed his eyes for a moment and opened them again. Then he snapped upright and whipped the gaderffii stick from behind his back, sweeping Cad Bane's legs out from under him in a single fluid move. As Bane hit the ground with a grunt of surprise, Fett knocked the mercenary's pistol away and glared down at him.

"I knew . . . you were . . . a killer," Bane said. He jerked his arm upward to shoot another jet of flame, but Fett deflected the attack with the staff. He hoisted the gaderffii stick up and thrust the sharp end through Cad Bane's chest, pinning him to the ground.

Bane gasped, and his body fell still. His hat lay next to him in the street.

Boba Fett turned and walked away.

THIRTY-THREE

NOT FAR AWAY, the Mods and Freetowners were firing blasters at the rancor as it continued its rampage through the city. Roaring, it stood on top of a building with a landspeeder in its hand. It flung the speeder down at the crowd below, scattering them, as the Mandalorian ran up the street.

"Put your blasters down!" he shouted. "Stop shooting!"

With a howl, the rancor turned and began to claw its way up to the top of a nearby tower. Its long arms pulled it upward as its claws ripped chunks of the structure away, destroying more of the tower with every blow.

Down below, Mando handed the child off to Peli. "Keep him safe," he said.

"Who's gonna keep *me* safe?" Peli asked.

"Here," Mando said, giving the child the metal ball

he'd taken from the control lever of the *Razor Crest*. "Hang on to this. It's gonna be okay."

Jetting upward, Mando landed on top of the rancor's back, but the creature plucked him off and smashed his body through the roof of the tower.

"Don't worry, kid," Peli told Grogu. "Your old man's crafty." She watched as the rancor grabbed Mando and jammed him into its mouth, the monster's teeth coming down on the Mandalorian's helmet. "Oof, spoke too soon."

Firing his flamethrower into the rancor's mouth, Mando twisted free of its teeth, only to have the creature hurl him backward into the street.

Peli clutched Grogu protectively while the majordomo cowered behind her. With a ground-shaking crash, the rancor landed in front of them. Leaning forward, it opened its mouth and claws, roaring into the faces of Peli and the majordomo, who both screamed back at it.

As the rancor turned to lumber toward Mando's fallen body, Peli said, "Don't worry, kid." She glanced down and saw that Grogu was gone. "Where'd you go, kid?"

She looked around and saw that the child was waddling out into the middle of the street to stand in front of the Mandalorian. Grogu looked up at the rancor, whose bellowing roar blew the child's ears back with the force of its breath.

Grogu raised one hand slowly toward the beast. Little by little, the rancor grew calmer and began to lower its head onto the street as its eyes drifted shut. A moment later it began to snore. Reaching up, Grogu touched the great creature's head. Then he sat down next to it, exhausted by the effort of putting it to sleep.

Peli walked over to the Mandalorian and helped him to his feet as they looked over at the rancor and the child.

"I'm guessing there's not gonna be a barbecue," she said.

THIRTY-FOUR

INSIDE THE DESERT Survey Office, the Pyke boss briefed the other members of the families on his plans. "The Syndicate forces have pulled back from Mos Espa," he said, "and should be arriving here in Mos Eisley shortly so that we may disembark."

"You can't just cut and run," one of the faction heads said. "We lost soldiers, too."

"We had a deal," Dokk Strassi added.

"Our deal was that Tatooine was going to be a hospitable place to do business," the Pyke reminded them, his voice tense. "Half of my men were either shot or eaten by a rancor. Is that what you call hospitable?"

Distant gunshots interrupted the discussion, and the room's inhabitants stopped and looked up. "Guards!" the Pyke boss ordered, but there was no response.

Everyone leapt up, weapons at the ready. Before they could react further, a series of quick blaster shots took each of them out, leaving only the Pyke boss and Mok Shaiz. A noose slipped down from above, encircling the mayor's long neck, and jerked him off his feet so he dangled from the ceiling.

Alone and panting with fear, the Pyke boss shot randomly at the ceiling, then stopped and listened. An instant later he gasped as an assassin's blade pierced his back. He fell forward and collapsed to the floor.

Fennec Shand rose up behind him. She took a quick glance at the bodies scattered around the room, then ran for the door.

THIRTY-FIVE

PEACE HAD RETURNED to Mos Espa. While starliners arrived and departed from the spaceport, Boba Fett and Fennec Shand walked the streets of the city, listening to the sounds of rebuilding. The people looked up and acknowledged Fett's passing with bows of respect and gratitude.

Nodding to them, Fett gestured with his arm in a traditional posture of welcome and winced in pain. He was still healing from the recent battle. "Why does it have to be the right arm?" he murmured.

"You should take a nice soak in the bacta tank," Fennec said.

"It's being used." He nodded to a group of workers who stopped what they were doing to bow. "Why must everyone bow at me?"

"It's better than shooting."

Fett looked bemused. "Are those my only two choices?"

"When you run the town it is," Fennec said. A group of children approached to offer them meiloorun fruit, and Fett took one.

"Thank you," he said, and when the children ran off, he looked over at Fennec. "We are not suited for this."

"If not us, then who?"

Before he could respond, Fett saw Krrsantan and the remaining Mods coming to meet them. Fett tossed the meiloorun fruit to the Wookiee, who caught it and took an appreciative bite.

"So the Wookiee gets a melon and we don't?" Skad asked.

Fennec looked up at the former gladiator. "Krrsantan, you want to share?"

The Wookiee growled, and the others joined together in laughter as they stood in the street. It was shaping up to be a beautiful day.

THIRTY-SIX

FLYING THROUGH SPACE away from Tatooine, the Mandalorian heard a familiar tapping coming from the dome behind him, where Grogu sat in his customized seat pod.

"No," he said.

The tapping came again, more insistent this time, as Grogu knocked his metal ball against the glass.

"Uh-uh," Mando said.

Tap-tap-tap.

"No."

Tap-tap-tap-tap!

Sighing, Mando turned to look at the wrinkled face and large dark eyes gleaming at him with anticipation. "All right," he said. "But this is the last time." He reached down to the N-1's console and flipped a switch. The child squealed in delight, hands in the air, as the ship accelerated with super-boosted speed and threw him back in his seat.

An instant later, they were gone.

In the back room of Boba's palace, Cobb Vanth lay in the bacta tank, soaking and recovering from his wounds. The healing would take time, and certain cybernetic repairs would need to be made.

Standing next to the tank, the Modifier began to prepare his tools.